Superseeds

For all who dream of alternative worlds

Also by Geoffrey Beevers and published by Fantom

THE FORGOTTEN FIELDS
THE PROGRESS ROAD

PREFACE

THIS BOOK DESCRIBES AN IMPOSSIBLE 'LOVE STORY' between two scientists across the barriers of Time.

It was completed in the very early 1990s, before the Internet, and before mobile phones and personal computers were in common use. The Cold War had just ended and Western capitalism seemed to have triumphed worldwide. It reflects the language and ideas of that time. It explores the possibility of bridging the gap between that 'present' and an imaginary future in 2050.

For me, time travel always seems too easy in fiction. I've tried to imagine how difficult it might be in reality, so the book becomes partly about the obsession to reach the unreachable.

The book is also about the science of genetic engineering. At the time GM food seemed altogether a bad idea ('Frankenstein Foods!'); but as I researched, I came to realise that it was not the science itself that was the problem, but the way it was used. The idea of a global corporation which could capture a technology and impose a monopoly on the world seemed to me a real danger. Now, half way between 1990 and 2050, in the age of the tech giants, and with natural diversity declining everywhere, the warning still feels relevant.

Geoffrey Beevers
August 2018

CHAPTER ONE

THEN ALL AT ONCE IT WAS COMPLETE.

The telephone immediately startled him.

'Hello Joe. Haven't you finished yet?'

'Nearly, I'm on the last paragraph.' Why had he lied? It was complete.

'It's Friday night. You've missed your deadline.'

'That's all right. I can deliver it on Monday morning.'

'How long will you be?'

Joe's mind wouldn't focus on such a simple question.

'Er... not long... say, half an hour.'

'Oh, brilliant. Then you'll come over. It's at Queens' at 9.30.'

'Well, I've got to go home first. I've nothing to wear.'

'Rubbish. Come as you are. The scatty boffin look is in. If you're like me you have to dress to kill – but if you're a genius, who cares what you look like – the girls go for it.'

'Sod off.'

Joe put the receiver down, got up and wandered around the little room, his mind elsewhere, absently pulling at his brown jacket. Then, all at once, he moved back to his desk and looked down at his neatly stacked papers.

It was finished. It was really and truly complete. He had been working twelve hours a day for as long as he could remember, in the labs and growth rooms, in the field and then writing up the research. And now he watched himself childishly putting in the last full stop, picking up the sheaf of papers and putting them together with his brief bibliography. It was finished and he was exhausted, feeling almost outside his body, looking down on himself. He was sliding the precious papers carefully into a folder now, and placing them into his desk drawer. He knew without question it was brilliant work. When the paper was published it would cause a scientific storm. But though he'd written it up well, the real proof was down there in the labs and growth rooms where his maize plants were growing tall. Every passing day confirmed an unmistakeable triumph. In controlled semi-arid conditions, the seeds had grown into strong disease-resistant plants, quietly fixing nitrogen from the air. Mixing and matching genes, he and his team had created a marvel, a living masterpiece to feed the world. It was finished, his creation was complete and he felt almost like a god. It was the end of the sixth day and it felt good. He shut his desk drawer and left the room, locking the door behind him.

It was still daylight as he emerged from the lab buildings and by the waft of warm air he guessed that it must have been a hot day. He cut the corner across the grass as he always did, between the shrubs; and, leaving the labs behind him, took the long straight driveway down to Huntingdon Road, before cutting through on his familiar route towards the city centre.

Dusk was falling as he followed the path across the grass to the wooden bridge over the Cam. There were only a few pink clouds in the sky deepening to indigo, and a fresh smell of growing things rose warmly all about him. As he crossed the river he turned back for a moment; and the sky, where the sun had set, stood in a peaceful glory behind him. Not far away at the edge of the water, he noticed a sleepy butterfly moving in a young lilac tree, heavy with scent. And the thought passed through his mind of the butterfly effect – the idea that one stroke of a butterfly's wings could have a cumulative effect which might create a tornado in another part of the world. It seemed an unlikely theory at the moment: the butterfly seemed too delicate and the summer weather so perfect and safe. It was hard to imagine Chaos; the evening was so complete, and he was in love with completion.

At Queens' College, Tony was already waiting for him just inside the porter's lodge, and Carol too. They were leaning against the stone wall, holding hands.

'Hello, me old mate,' said Tony. 'Did you get it done then?' Joe grinned.

'The party's over there,' said Carol, grinning back and pointing across the courtyard.

'In the History Tutor's rooms,' said Tony and winked enigmatically. 'History is being made tonight!'

A bass rhythm thumped into the courtyard in the gathering dark. On the knocker of the wooden door, two yellow and blue balloons were tied, as if welcoming them to a children's party.

Joe led the way up the ancient wooden staircase. Tony and Carol followed, pausing for a kiss on the landing. Tony had told them it was just a small party for the company who had helped fund his research, just to mark the end of his research phase. Joe hadn't given it a great deal of thought. He knew that his research team would be there: Carol of course, but also Peter, Anne-Marie, Jimbo and the rest; perhaps a few stuffed-shirted chaps from PCCI.

But surprisingly, it was very crowded. They stood near the door.

'I thought you said it was just a small party for your PCCI people.'

'We thought a celebration was in order,' said Tony. 'Did you hear the patents are all lined up? I'm off to Egypt in a couple of weeks to see what interest I can get going. Cairo, then Addis Ababa, Nairobi. Things are really beginning to move. Where have you put your research? You've not dropped it in the river I hope?' And he looked at Joe with mock horror.

'No, don't worry, it's all locked up.'

Tony peered into the crowded, swaying room. Somewhere there was the noise of a released champagne cork and a cry of appreciation. Carol slipped away to get some drinks for them.

'Let me just survey this talent,' Tony said, then: 'God, there are some stunning birds here tonight. You've been buried in that office den of yours for so long you must be feeling like a rampant monk on sabbatical. Here, come and meet the lovely Gilda. Gilda, this is Joe, the boffin who made all this possible. He's all ready to publish. Oh, Sarah, this is Joe.'

'Hello.'

Joe became aware that half the room was turning towards him, watching him as he shook hands with the long-legged creatures who looked like models. They looked far too adoringly at him, so that he felt self-conscious. There was more noise all around him than he'd heard in weeks. A party streamer rose above the crowd. A glass was put into his hand.

'You must have a drink,' Sarah was saying.

'It must be a bit boring, buried at a desk all day,' some man in a suit was saying, but he didn't look as if he spent long away from a far more boring desk himself.

'Is it a relief to be released?' Gilda was asking.

'Well, I prefer practical research,' he found himself saying, 'but it's very satisfying to find that I... er...'

Suddenly he was aware of being at the centre of a group of people who were all listening to him. The sensation was very unusual. He realised that he hadn't had a real conversation with anyone for weeks. He could remember going to very few parties since he and Tony had been undergraduates together, nine or ten years ago. He felt inadequate, as if everyone expected wise words of him and he couldn't provide them.

People had been dancing when he came in. Now they seemed to have stopped.

Suddenly the music stopped too, and a soft Scottish voice said, 'Hello everybody. For those of you who don't know me, the name's McAndrew. You probably know me as Mac – but if you don't, I'm the research director of PCCI here in Britain. I'd like to thank Professor... um... Professor Thomson for the loan of these beautiful university rooms for this party.'

There were a lot of cries of 'Thank you!' and raised glasses.

McAndrew was a tall ginger-haired man who always wore

a tie, and always looked uncomfortable in it – as if his collars were too small. He had a tired, greying moustache. But he was known for being a clever man.

He had got up on a chair at the far end of the room. 'And now I'd like to introduce someone in whose honour we are meeting tonight. Although he doesn't know it yet.' There was laughter. 'A very special scientist and a very special man. Joe Goodman.'

Everybody turned towards Joe and clapped.

'This is Your Life,' someone quipped.

'And he's only thirty,' laughed another.

Joe wanted to run away. Tony had never warned him of this. He looked for Tony among all the faces, but he seemed to have disappeared. Joe took a gulp from his glass and tried to smile.

'I don't want to embarrass you Joe,' said Mac, 'but for those of you laymen in the agribusiness world who aren't aware of what's been going on, I'd just like to say that the race has been on for some time to come up with improved seeds to feed the hungry of the world. But while some companies we know have concentrated on coated seeds which will go hand in hand with the use of their own brands of pesticides and the new post-emergent broad-spectrum herbicides, we've taken a different course. We've gone for the big one!'

There were appreciative murmurs around the room, which collapsed into slightly drunken idiocy in one corner.

'I hope there are no industrial spies among us…' said Mac.

'Shame!' came the cry.

'… because I'm talking about the search for a very special new seed. Something that will truly revolutionise agriculture. This seed is not only engineered to be pest resistant, drought resistant and with many other genetic advantages, but this seed can do without fertiliser... this seed can fix its own nitrogen from the air.'

In the silence that followed, Mac dropped his voice. 'Now I don't need to tell you the cost of nitrogen fertiliser. A year or two ago – in 1990, I think it was – the world was already spending fifteen billion on nitrogen fertiliser, not to mention the associated cost of storage and equipment and transport; and think how those costs affect a Third World country already desperately in debt, and in need of hospitals and schools. It also costs three tons of oil to produce one ton of fertiliser and think how this affects the world's scarce resources. Then again, it's been well publicised how the run-off from nitrates can pollute the underground water tables. Well, this new seed would mean an eventual goodbye to all those problems.'

He paused briefly.

'Now I don't understand all the scientific details of how this wonder seed might be produced – so don't ask me...' There was laughter again now at his mock-innocence, and Mac lifted his voice above it. '... but I'm told that it's something to do with the genes from the rhizobia bacteria, and that it's a very complicated process involving splicing as many as seventeen genes. But it seems that the scientists on Joe's team, working over here at the Biotechnology Centre, and with our help and our financial backing, have now come up with the answer –'

There were claps and cheers from everywhere, and again everybody looked at Joe.

'Yes, the seeds have been created, the plants are growing well, the results are to be published next week – isn't that right, Joe?'

'Yes,' nodded Joe.

'And thanks to the new European directives, all the relevant patents are ours.'

He said this with unusual relish, and there were more claps, especially from the men in suits in one corner, who, Joe guessed, were probably the lawyers of PCCI.

'Now I'm not going to pretend there's nothing in it for us,' Mac continued, running his finger round his collar. 'The sole right to sell Joe's seed all over the world will prove of great long-term benefit to our company, even though we may lose chemical sales in the mid term, and it's obvious that our fertiliser subsidiaries may suffer in particular. But we're sure to corner a huge future market and we expect to make quite a profit on it overall. There's nothing wrong with profit. But that's not our chief satisfaction tonight. Let's put aside for a moment our personal and corporate considerations, and take a more foresighted view – what we may call a "green" view of things…'

There was more clapping, so that Mac had to pause before going on.

'By the year 2050, there will be billions of extra mouths to feed, mostly living in Third World cities. And now it really does look as if we may have discovered a seed to enable the Third World to feed its hungry populations more cheaply; and surely there could be no finer ambition than that. Seeds are a powerful symbol of the future, but what we have now is what we might call a Superseed – a symbol of a great future, that we could never before have dreamt of, even in our wildest dreams. A future of co-operation between the rich and the poor worlds. Imagine a future without famine, where every human being on this planet has enough to eat, so that every man's capacities can be used to the full, and not blighted by malnutrition and disease. And for making this dream a real possibility we have to thank you, Joe, for your brilliance and dedication. If there's any justice you should receive the Nobel Prize for this discovery – though in the way of things,' he joked, 'that may not be next week.' He waited for the laughter to die down.

'But in the meantime, let's just be glad to be here tonight. One day people may say to each other, "Where were you when the Superseed was invented?" Well, we were here. We, who were lucky enough to be in at the beginning, who thought we'd gather here to mark the moment, and to give our thanks to you Joe. So let's toast – Joe Goodman!'

Everybody turned to Joe and raised their glasses. He felt very foolish, and smiled and raised his glass too. Some people cried 'Speech, speech!' and a silence fell. He was somehow standing in the centre of the room. He looked around. All eyes were on him.

'Er…' he faltered. 'I'm really not prepared and I'm… Oh… God…'

He stopped and then took a deep breath and started again.

'It's not just me, it's all the team. Come out of there!' he said, gesturing towards the group by the leather-topped desk in the window. He could see Carol, and the mop of hair over Jimbo's eyes; Anne-Marie looking quite different in make-up, and one or two others. He tried to encourage them to join him but they refused. He muttered something else about other teams, and backup, but he knew he was behaving idiotically, in the manner of a film actor receiving an Oscar. He tried to say that Mac had been exaggerating somewhat, and then he said, 'Let me give you another toast. Um. Let's drink to what we seem to have nicknamed the Superseed. I'm sure there's a long way to go yet.'

'Don't be too cautious,' someone put in, trying to help.

'Typical scientist!' called out someone from the back, and there was laughter.

'Well, we've still got field trials in different countries and so on. Several years yet. But let's drink to it, and that it may live up to the hopes of all of us in the future. The Superseed.'

And everybody raised their glasses and cried 'Superseed!' and Joe hurried off to find Tony to blame him for landing him in this mess.

'You bastard,' he said. And for the first time that evening Joe took in Tony's clothes, the fashionable cream suit and party shirt. 'And look at you,' he went on while Tony laughed. 'I must be the only person wearing a T-shirt and an old jacket.'

'Nobody minds,' said Tony. 'Here, sit down and have another drink. You should be well chuffed. That was a good speech. Sit down. How are you feeling?'

Somebody else moved for him quickly and Joe, still protesting, found himself sitting next to Tony on the sofa.

'I don't know yet. I've only just finished writing it up. This is all too quick. I haven't really surfaced yet.'

'You should savour your success. God knows you've achieved enough.'

'I expect someone else's team would have got there if we hadn't.'

'Then it was a race, and you won. Enjoy the gold medal. No prizes for dreaming up the double helix the day after Watson and Crick have published.'

'Oh come on, it's not like that.'

'Course it is. Anyway I've got to believe it. I'm off to sell it to the Africans.' Tony rubbed his hands together in genuine glee. 'Protected by patent. I can't wait. Wicked!'

'How long are you going to be in Egypt?'

'I think a week or two initially. Set up as many meetings as I can.' He leaned forward and took a bottle from the coffee table in front of them and then went on, 'This is going to be a world best-seller. Here, have another drink. We're a great partnership, you and I; you develop the ideas and I'll sell them. We'll make a fortune. Mind you, I wish I had a percentage. Have you? God, this is not very good wine is it? Did I tell you I had a girlfriend in Cairo?'

'I thought you'd sworn undying love to Carol.'

'Oh, did she tell you that?' Tony seemed suddenly to have sobered. 'Well I did. And I meant it, really. The girl in Cairo's nothing important.' He took another drink. 'But boy, is she beautiful. Cool.' He leaned forward and whispered, 'Wrap her legs around your neck as soon as look at you. Pardon the expression. When are you going to meet a new girl?'

'Give me a chance. I've been buried in the lab for weeks.'

'Well now's your opportunity! You've got brains, success, good looks – all the aphrodisiacs; look at those grey, bedroom eyes…'

Joe grinned.

'Time to cash in,' said Tony. 'Reap the rewards.'

'You've got a one-track mind,' said Joe.

'No, you're the obsessive. Buried in the lab. No wonder Jill got bored. Oh sorry, sore point.'

Joe thought of Jilly. She had become so dependent on him, but yet she'd not been able to share his thoughts on his research, and he'd had no other thoughts for months. He felt guilty. He remembered her pain on parting, and even then he'd not been able to leave his desk to comfort her.

'What are you going to do next?' Tony was asking.

'I don't know. Get the research to the publisher on Monday. Er… I don't know. Take a bit of a break for a week or two, I suppose. I haven't really thought.'

'The trouble with you is, you live in your head too much. You should take Sarah here off to the Bahamas.' He called out to Sarah: 'Come and join us.' As she came over, Joe filled his glass from a bottle on the table.

'Sarah, do you want to go to the Bahamas?'

Sarah considered Tony's question suspiciously. 'Why?'

'Because Joe would like to take you.'

'Joe?' said Sarah smiling, and Joe laughed.

'What do you think of his T-shirt?' said Tony.

'It's rather sweet,' said Sarah.

'What did I tell you?' said Tony.

Sarah sat between them on the sofa and they all talked. After a while the music started again and Joe and Sarah danced where others were dancing, crushed into the middle of the room. She was attractive but already his head was beginning to swim. He felt happy but disconnected from himself. The world was too bright for him; he felt like a mole in the sunlight. He decided he would go soon, and so he searched out Professor Thomson to say goodbye. But the Professor didn't seem to have been invited to this party.

He went over to say goodbye to Mac, but Mac was already surrounded by two or three acolytes. They made way for Joe respectfully.

'Just how badly is this discovery expected to hit our fertiliser sales?' one of them was asking Mac. 'Aren't HQ a bit worried? I'd never really thought much about that before.'

Neither had Joe.

'I wouldn't lose any sleep,' said Mac. 'Between ourselves PCCI are already at an advanced stage of selling off our fertiliser interests. All at a very good price. After all, it's one of the most profitable assets of the business.' He paused. 'Till next week of course, Joe. Then everybody'll want to get out...' He smiled slyly.

Joe could see his point. But he'd been too busy making his breakthrough to worry about killings to be made on international share markets. He started to move on.

'Come and see me on Monday,' said Mac and shook him warmly by the hand to the envy of others. 'We must arrange for you to meet the press.'

After that Joe felt he must talk to Peter and Anne-Marie and the rest of his team. They all seemed to be having such fun and soon they'd persuaded him to stay after all. Then he met Ivan Davitsky, the resident psychologist at PCCI who always looked to him so like the cliché of the Eastern European psychologist, and with whom he sometimes enjoyed long conversations like this one about Jung and synchronicity. 'Synchronicity involves no causality,' Davitsky was saying intensely, 'it's a random phenomenon, so one should never assign significance to an unlikely meeting between...' But now Joe couldn't concentrate. He suddenly became surrounded by the suited brigade from PCCI again and found himself trying to express the technicalities of gene-splicing or cloning with tissue-culture techniques. He felt no intolerance now as he might normally have felt. Everywhere he met praise and respect and friend-ship, and his glass was continually refilled. He got into a conversation about whether the Tories could win the next election without Thatcher, and a little later a man in a suit was saying, 'It's far too early to say if global warming is real – it could be simply random weather patterns.'

And suddenly this gawky young student was talking about whales. His long fingers flickered about expressively as he explained how much bigger a whale's brain was than a man's. Man had developed a brain because of his hands, but how and why had whales developed all this brain when they had no hands?

'No hands!' he said, throwing his hands in the air.

Joe found himself strangely impressed by this, though he realised how much the wine had gone to his head. Now the boy was talking about how whales make love. Somehow, it seemed, they chose their mates at a distance, picking each other individually in spite of the most impossible distances, vast tracts of oceans. They sought each other out, racing towards each other, communicating all the time, singing their songs. What a sophisticated system of communication they must have, the boy was saying; and when they finally meet, he was saying, and his eyes were opened wide, 'Then they come together,' and he brought his palms together, 'and they rise up through the water and explode into the sky with sheer joy...' He demonstrated with his long hands high above his head.

But then Gilda drew Joe away, and he was dancing again, with Sarah and Anne-Marie and one or two others. Later, as he sat on the sofa, he noticed Tony, entwined with Carol in a corner behind him. Then he was watching, fascinated, as a party balloon, filled with gas but slightly puckered, rose slowly, so slowly, above the crowd, till it stuck on the ceiling. It was long, and red, and sausage shaped. It seemed to hesitate there, unsure of whether to stay up there or come down.

'Like me, when I've had too much to drink,' Tony was whispering in his ear, but by the time Joe turned round he was back with Carol in the corner, laughing, and someone else was sitting beside him on the sofa, looking at him with exaggerated respect. He remembered feeling almost disembodied, like the balloon. Then suddenly he was aware that the party was thinning out. He remembered kissing some girls goodbye, and taking some telephone numbers and then waving across the room, where people responded warmly – was that Ivan Davitsky? – and then at nearly two o'clock he spilled out on to the street to find his way home.

And all at once he felt again that huge sense of release. It was a warm, balmy night with a bright moon shining. There had been months, years of work. He had been submerged in detail, with so many blocks, eventually overcome, so many months of frustration and near-despair. But now, all at once, the job was done. It was finished. He felt an extraordinary sense of joy, of being complete, fulfilled. The Superseed. He found himself smiling ridiculously to himself in the moonlight. The Superseed.

On his way home, he found himself in the centre of the deserted city. He felt really quite drunk and wished he had eaten more. He could hear the click of his shoes as he walked down the middle of the road, echoing back from the deserted shop fronts, a rather uneven sound. The moon behind cast a thin shadow in front of him, as he turned left at the end of Downing Street and walked through the centre, passing Boots and then Marks and Spencer and Woolworths. Then, in the dark, he suddenly found himself jumping in the air, with the sheer joy of excitement, and punching his fist at the stars, like a footballer after scoring a goal.

'Yes,' he found himself shouting. 'Yes!'

And then 'Success!'

And then he felt self-conscious. He was glad it was the middle of the night and no one could see him.

A lover of cinema, when he had the time, he was drawn down Market Passage to the Arts Cinema, and soon found himself looking intently at the stills outside. It must be the summer holidays, he thought, as Walt Disney's *Fantasia* was on again; there were pictures of pink elephants. And there was a picture which especially took his eye, of many animated brooms carrying pails of water on a stairway. He had seen the film once and tried to remember it. Somehow the brooms were relentless, bringing help in the form of endless pails of unwanted water, conjured up by a junior wizard who didn't know what he was doing. Mickey Mouse. He remembered enjoying the film.

He moved on, up Sidney Street. He needed something to eat, badly. Amazingly, at such a late hour, there was a light on over a shop down the road.

Ben's Beefburger Bar.

A new chippie must have opened. He went carefully up the road and into the shop.

'We're just closing,' said the man behind the counter.

There was a silence. Joe just stood there swaying slightly.

'What do you want?' said the man.

'Just a bag of chips,' said Joe.

The man sighed.

'Great,' he said heavily. 'Last order tonight.' He dipped the chips into the oil. He waited for them to brown.

'I don't know why I do this,' said the man at last. 'It's a treadmill.'

There was a pause.

'I don't have to do it,' he said.

Another pause.

'Always someone comes along, just when you're closing.'

A long pause. Then he took the chips out and handed them to Joe. He took the money, closed the oil-vat, put off a light, took up a broom to sweep the floor. He left no doubt that he was closing.

'Thank you,' said Joe, and left.

'Thank you,' the man grumbled, sarcastically, 'thank you very, very much.'

And as he went down the street Joe could still hear the man's grumbles.

'The food business,' Joe just caught him saying, 'it's a killer...'

The chips did little to sober Joe. He still felt euphoric, and restless. He didn't want to go home. He suddenly had the desire to go back to the labs to see his plants growing, to look at his completed research. He wondered why. Was he so obsessed that he couldn't leave it alone? Or was it just for comfort? No, he just wanted to celebrate its completion. He had hardly had time to think yet. He headed back to the labs, up Huntingdon Road.

At the end of the long straight drive bordered by lawns and shrubs, there stood a long, low, red-brick building, functional but durable. The offices were in the three-storey block to the right, and the labs and greenhouses were spread out to the left with a deceptively large space at the back for field testing. The labs were almost windowless, lit mainly by skylights from above. He wondered where Einstein had been the evening after he'd finally put together the Theory of Relativity. Or Newton, after his Theory of Gravity was finally complete. Surely somewhere more glamorous than this.

The whole place seemed deserted. He found his keys, unlocked the doors and went in. Beyond the empty reception desk he turned left and found his way along the corridor. It was lit by moonlight from above. Down a few steps, he unlocked another door and turned on the light.

It was fairly long and spacious as labs go, with a clock on the wall at the end. At workbenches on either side there were microscopes, UV scanners and computer screens, tubes and other jars of seeds, circular trays full of nutrient jelly, all the paraphernalia of the lab, all scattered in the usual working mess. On the walls were cupboards and charts, and postcards where Anne-Marie worked, and some pin-ups for Jimbo. Further down the lab, a dividing semi-partition jutted out into the room, with tier upon tier of shelves stacked with propagators and seed trays and other equipment, and here and there young plants thrusting up. Beyond the partition could be dimly seen the door which led to the growth rooms.

He walked down the silent lab and, passing the partition, turned right and unlocked the door. The corridor beyond seemed warm, dimly lit by moonlight from a door at the end, which led into the greenhouses. He opened the doors to one or two of the growth rooms to look inside. In the first were some plants glowing in the dark, marked as they were by a 'glow-worm' gene to indicate the success of a particular transfer. They were a beautiful sight, their fragile forms branching brightly in the darkness. A little further down the corridor was a sight more beautiful still. When he turned on the light for a moment, there were his maize cultivars growing strong and luxuriant, the scent of growth heavy in the warm and concentrated air. He felt a thrill of pleasure as he sampled the growth rooms, walking down to the end and back, looking at them. For once he rejoiced in the indulgence.

As he came back into the cooler air of the labs he was already beginning to speculate on the future. Would he get an irresistible offer from PCCI? Or would there be more money available now for research here, he wondered. What would these labs look like in ten years' time? How would the 'Superseed' be viewed then? If he was honest with himself, he had been flattered by Mac's speech. Was all this really worth a Nobel Prize, and could it really mean a future without famine? Perhaps, he thought, if he could look further into the future and really see the world as it would be in the 2050s, then… and all at once he stood stock-still and felt a chill crawl up the back of his neck.

Out of the corner of his eye he had caught the suspicion of a movement. Somewhere there, dimly glimpsed through the tiers of propagators and seed trays between him and the way out, was a movement. He felt a strange expectation. Could it have been a mouse or some other animal? He stood and watched in silence. Again he felt something had moved at the far end of the lab. As he ducked down now to get a better view, he glimpsed through the racks a girl standing with her back to him.

His first thought was, how could she possibly have got in? She was slender and tall, almost gawky, and had short hair, a long neck, and tight, fair curls. She was wearing black: loose black trousers, and some kind of strangely cut black top. She seemed to be absorbed by something at the workbench. Carol might have come back, or one of the team, or even one of the undergraduate students who gave their help, but Carol had dark hair and in any case it was strange because the doors had been locked until a moment ago. He turned back carefully to shut the door to the greenhouses, but the door clicked as he locked it. He turned as quickly and quietly as he could into the lab. But when he looked up, the girl had gone.

He walked back through the lab, up the steps into the corridor and stopped to listen. Where was she? It was absolutely silent up there. He went back and carefully checked the lab again and then came out, turned off the light and locked the door. He turned on no more lights but moved on quietly through the patches of moonlight. He was puzzled, wondering if it had been some kind of hallucination. He had been working very hard for many days, and he had just had too little to eat and too much to drink. Yet the girl had seemed so real, so entirely herself, her hair and her odd clothes so exactly remembered.

He decided he must have been seeing things. The obsessions of work, followed by the party and the fact that he had not had time to stop in between, had affected his mind. He was beginning to feel sober again now. He felt very alone and suddenly and quite inexplicably sad.

It was only a few months since he had broken up with Jilly. His own obsessive nature had been to blame. He increasingly seemed to put himself in positions where he was on his own.

He found himself mechanically trudging up the stairs to open up his little office. He turned on the desk lamp and opened the drawer of his desk. His research was still there, safe and sound. For some reason he moved it into one of the metal filing cabinets, and put it at the back in a rarely used and unusual place. Then he locked it up and put the little key in his pocket. He sat at his desk for a moment, the place where he had spent so much of his time in the last few weeks. Then a wave of exhaustion claimed him. He crossed his arms on the desk in front of him and laid his head on his arms. He couldn't face the thought now of walking all the way home. It was finished. It was complete. He felt amazed at everything, by his success, by everything. His mind was hardly functioning. He felt very tired. Why should he worry about the future?

Surely he deserved to sleep now.

And so he slept.

Why should he dream about the future?

A flat desert. Hot sun on his face. He was standing alone, on a high podium decorated with bright bunting, and to his left some African villagers had gathered. There were tents, and families were gathering in groups. There were some cheers and clapping. They were all looking out across the desert which stretched in front of them as far as the eye could see. On his right, a band was playing 'The Sorcerer's Apprentice' and Joe sensed a movement on the horizon. On the rim of the desert, at the far edge of sight, sprang up a line of coloured balloons.

They popped up cheerfully through the sand on long strings, balloons of red and yellow and blue, filling the desert with colour. In rows they sprang up, one in front of the other, as well spaced as plants in a seed bed, spreading across the desert towards him, swinging on their strings to the beat like the brooms with the pails of water in the Walt Disney film, marching nearer and nearer across the plain. As they drew near, the villagers fell silent and then they scattered and ran. Suddenly the giant balloons were all about him and were spreading on behind him to the horizon. Somewhere in their shadow, the band was playing on.

Now he wanted to get down off the podium; but it was much higher that it had been: it seemed a long way up and the only way down was a staircase at the back. It was thin, and curved back and forth. It was iron, like a fire escape. As he started to descend, the thick skins of the balloons started to burst flabbily all around him, collapsing into floppy rubber flowers. The balloons were deflating into soggy rubber. And now there was the sound of flames from below. Pieces of ironwork were breaking off in his hand; steps of the fire escape were missing. He grew more fearful, his way more painfully slow.

At last the fire escape ended in mid-air. There were flames below. He jumped. Now he was on the ground and there was devastation. Burnt stubble everywhere, steaming, the aftermath of a great fire. A few fallen shreds of shrivelled rubber, a party streamer or two. He started to walk across the hot sandy ground, puzzled. Was he looking for something? He found himself thinking: Where are the whales? They've bigger brains than we have. And then a moment later thinking, How can there be whales in the desert? He found himself longing for water. He seemed to be walking a long way. It was a wide desert, not an oasis in sight.

Then, out of the corner of his eye, he caught the suspicion of a movement. At first he thought it must be some desert animal, but he turned slowly as if he knew to expect something important. Some twenty yards away stood the girl he had seen in the lab, her back to him. She was bending over a cracked hole in the earth and was looking into it. She dropped on to her knees in front of it. There was something in the hole, but he didn't dare look into it too. But in spite of himself, he started to move towards her. He saw again her black clothes, her short curly hair and her long white neck strangely untouched by the sun. As he came close, she looked up, startled. He saw that she had been crying bitterly. Was she blaming him for something?

They looked at each other for what seemed a long time. Or rather, time seemed to empty out of the moment. It was beyond time.

The hot desk-lamp shone in his face. His mind was full of some unexplained question. The sensation was familiar. If he could only bring the question into definition, an answer could not be far away. But somehow, as with all dreams, the question was slipping away. He sat up. His desk was empty. Somewhere a clock was ticking; time was filling up again. But otherwise the silence was complete.

It was time to go home.

But as he walked slowly home, the girl at least stayed in his mind. He could imagine her so clearly, conceive the whole of her life, almost as if she were real…

CHAPTER TWO

As she returned from the Goodman labs to her office desk, Kassy decided that her life was a total failure, an unfinished, frustrating, shapeless, impossible mess.

In fact, she'd really no idea why she'd wandered down to the labs just now. There was nothing she could do there. Nothing of use. She sat and stared hopelessly down while the late afternoon sun warmed the keyboard on her desk. She glanced around the office. It was the end of the day and her secretary had already gone home. She stared at the wall charts, where every gene in every major cereal crop was mapped. She stared at the entrance to the seed-storage rooms. There was nothing else she could do today. She was killing time now till the meeting.

She had been back on the videophone to Luis in Mexico, and had drawn a complete blank. All week she had been trying to trace a rare and ancient wild relative of the Superseed maize.

One of the scientists hoped to find a resistant gene in it, and of course the landrace variety LV143 had been in the base collection, in the cold room, in its proper place. But closer inspection had revealed that it hadn't been grown out for twenty years, and the results even then had been very poor indeed. And now she couldn't get a single plant to grow.

It was the old story: lack of money, other priorities, refrigeration failures during the 20s and 30s. She'd spent hours on the Supernet, connecting with other gene banks in the US and the Middle East, India and Asia, but had turned up nothing. The so-called 'in situ' protection areas were worse than useless, wiped out by climate change. Luis in Mexico had seemed the most hopeful avenue; LV143 had been successfully grown out there as little as ten years ago, according to the records, but now he could find no seeds that weren't contaminated by storage problems. She would have to be patient, see if any of her seeds would grow into plants. But now that they were needed, so few of the rarer seeds in her massive base collection seemed to be viable at all. And she must face the music again at the crisis meeting at six-thirty.

She felt sick with it. Everybody would want to blame her; no one would want her excuses. She felt like a librarian who knew the original value of every beautifully bound book in her collection, but whose books actually fell apart if you took them down from the shelves.

She stopped herself. Her mind was churning uselessly; she was staring at her cluttered desk like a zombie. She was tired, she told herself, she had been working such long hours. Why should she feel a failure? She was doing her best in the job she'd always wanted, in her father's firm. She'd got a good degree, if not the expected first, and a seat on the board at a very young age. Since she'd turned thirty she'd begun to suspect that she might never want to marry or have children; she feared too much the idea of losing control of her life. In fact, it was only a few weeks since she had broken up with Timothy; but she minded less than she thought she would. He had become too pushy and she needed space. She was content. Her father was an impossible autocrat of course, but she got on well with her brother, and she had some good friends.

And yet somewhere deep inside her, there was a sense of failure sitting in her like a stone, with a life of its own almost separate from hers; and round it churned a violent rage and depression and frustration that she couldn't understand. She felt like smashing something.

She was aware of the rush of feet in the corridor outside. Now the labs were emptying; it was the end of another working day. Her fingers punched up the television service on her computer screen and she stumbled into the middle of a current affairs programme. The sound was turned down but she knew what the arrows on the map of Russia meant, thrusting across the great plains at a hundred miles a day as if to illustrate a military campaign. And now the reporter was standing among the devastated ears of wheat. And now there were the endless queues for bread. And then, there it was again, she could hardly believe it: she had broken again into that desert world where the reporter seemed eternally to be picking his way through the starving bodies of children. The flies on the faces, the distended stomachs. The whole world seemed to be starving. She flicked it off, and paced the room feeling helpless and angry.

Abruptly she cut off her feelings and busied herself at her desk, sorting out the loose ends of the day. After a while she went down into the storage rooms to check all was well among the long lines of liquid nitrogen vats, the coldroom shelves and the tiers of metal cabinets. Unusually, none of her team was working late tonight, so she locked up. They must be exhausted, with all the recent pressures, all the demands on them. When she returned to her office, her computer was flashing to call her to the board meeting. She closed it down, gathered some papers, and locked up the office; then, security pass in hand, she left the lab buildings.

Walking down Huntingdon Road on her familiar route towards the city centre, Kassy came at last to Parkside where the great block of Superseed House dominated the open green, in the hideous style of the early part of the century. A huge green poster hung over the main doorway:

THE THIRD WORLD DEPENDS ON US

God help the Third World, she thought wryly, not for the first time.

There were security men in their green uniforms everywhere, as she took the lift up to her father's huge office on the thirteenth floor. On the double doors there was a brass sign.

JONAS WHITE
EXECUTIVE DIRECTOR
SUPERSEED (EUROPE)

Timothy was already waiting by the door, obviously hanging about for her, with a lost expression on his face. She smiled and hoped he wouldn't say anything personal to her.

She felt vulnerable enough as it was. Thankfully he simply opened the door for her, and then went on his own way across the boardroom. She felt guilty. They were almost the last to arrive. Several board members were dotted about chatting quietly while others were taking their seats at the long table. She joined Sam, the research director, and Peter from economics. They were edgy and self-absorbed.

'These crisis meetings are becoming routine,' said Peter.

'Can you have a routine crisis?' said Kassy, and Sam's dry laugh sounded like a cough.

Jonas was calling for attention, and everyone made for their chairs. Kassy felt even more nervous than usual as she took her place at the junior end of the table. Down at the other end Jonas was preparing to speak. With his glasses and high forehead, he looked more like an academic than a tycoon. Kassy guessed that he would probably begin by saying a few encouraging words about Superseed's place in history.

'Let's start,' he said, and silence fell immediately.

Kassy was not disappointed; her father rarely missed the opportunity to draw comfort from the past. Apart from running his huge empire, he'd commissioned a three-volume history of the corporation, the third volume of which was about to be published.

'I just want to say that it's not for nothing that the Superseed has established itself over the last fifty years as the dominant monoculture of the earth. Our research departments have always managed to keep up with the pace of change in nature, engineering seeds to survive the great blight and even the great climate changes of the 20s and 30s. But this time, if we don't find the answer to our present problems, millions of people who have come to depend on the Superseed varieties will quite simply starve to death. The situation is already a lot worse than last week, and worse even than you have seen on the news. The creature that the media have so unfortunately termed the "Superbug" is spreading rapidly, not only in a swathe through the northern food-belts, but has now even been found in South America and South Africa. Seventy per cent of wheat is being destroyed worldwide and fifty per cent of maize. A related mutation is attacking the rice crop. Without truly resistant seeds for the next years' planting, the situation will be more disastrous than any of us could envisage. Now I want an update on the political situation, on the state of research and I want to consider any lateral suggestions. The political situation please, John.'

Kassy felt the silence around the table as the political officer rose, and a tension in her stomach. The white-haired old man explained with the aid of computer maps how the great wheat-belts of Canada and Siberia would probably provide enough bread to feed the richer countries of the world, albeit at a subsistence level and at greatly increased prices; but there was no hope of feeding the poor countries through the winter to come. Food Aid would simply dry up. People were beginning to understand this, and bitter attacks were increasing daily on offices, research centres, storage facilities and transport links, in fact wherever the Superseed transnational presence was felt. This in turn was hampering the research so desperately needed. He went in some depth into the situation in Delhi.

'It's an increasingly black picture everywhere,' he concluded, 'but an announcement of a research breakthrough would certainly calm the immediate political situation.'

Jonas thanked his political officer and called on Jim, the chief scientist, to explain the situation in research.

Kassy admired Jim. He explained calmly and clearly all the research options, their advantages and disadvantages. There were no breakthroughs as yet. To genetically engineer this so-called 'Superbug' was proving impossible, as it was mutating so extraordinarily fast. Even the most sophisticated super-pheremones seemed to be ineffective. To engineer a predator might be possible, but to release it too hastily into the environment might be even more dangerous than the present situation. In the longer term, to genetically manipulate the seed for resistance seemed the most hopeful avenue to follow. But this would require exploration of new strains of wheat…

As he talked Kassy felt the blood drain out of her. She could feel eyes turning towards her, knew she would be asked in a moment to explain the backup that her base collection seed-bank could provide. She had only been in charge for two years and this crisis had only come to her door in the last few months. When her father had elevated her to the board, he had not expected her position at the basic gene pool to become so high-profile. He seemed a little embarrassed to call on her.

She stood up. Her heart was thumping.

'The problem,' she tried to explain, 'is that the genetic base of almost all the Superseed varieties has always been too narrow. We no longer have enough of the old varieties of plants to broaden that base.'

'Why not?' came Jonas's voice sharply from the other end of the table. In the face of her father's questioning she suddenly felt like a small child caught in some act of wrongdoing. She hated herself for it.

'I think it's because the Superseed has been so successful in the past, our genetic engineers have only needed a few "elite" varieties to back it up, so the less obvious or wilder or more ancient varieties have been overlooked. And now that we're trying to grow them again, most of them are extinct, or simply not viable.'

'Why is that?' the dry voice cracked down the table again. Much as he loved her, Jonas could not be seen to be soft on his own daughter.

'Because there's not been the money available to preserve them. And sometimes they've not stored well, or been grown out in the wrong environment. In the crisis of the 20s and 30s other things took precedence. More recently the Superseed crops have been so successful that nobody has seen the need…'

'Can't they find the seeds in the wild?' came Timothy's voice from halfway down the table. Was he trying to help her?

'Most of the natural habitats were wiped out after the turn of the century, especially during the climate changes in the 20s and 30s. And, of course, farmers are no longer allowed to breed varieties for themselves.'

'Well if your gene bank can't find what we need, can't we go to another?' came a sarcastic-sounding voice from somewhere else. Kassy felt she was fighting for her life. She told the story of today's search for LV143 round the gene banks of the world. After that there was a silence.

Jim came to her rescue. 'I'd like to point out,' he said, 'that there's no guarantee that any of these old varieties would provide an answer. They may not have any particularly useful gene. It's only a long shot. But we're obviously spending a lot of money now on the gene bank to test for viability and so

31

widen the gene pool we can work from. Unfortunately it's an expensive and slow process. And of course it doesn't solve our immediate problem.'

Kassy felt temporarily released from the spotlight, and she sat down. But for a minute or two she could hardly take in what others said. Though it was hardly her fault that the stock had been allowed to decay over half a century, in an irrational way she felt deeply responsible.

By the time she was able to listen clearly again, the debate had moved on. Encouraged by the mention of lateral thinking, someone had suggested the massive application of DDT and other old-fashioned pesticides, which because of their toxicity had not been used for decades. A split then developed between the ecological approach of the bioengineers and those supporting older and blunter remedies. And Kassy felt her nervousness arise again, as if she had something more to add to the debate, though she was not aware of what it was.

Soon a tall Kenyan, whom Kassy didn't know, rose to his feet opposite her and made an earnest plea for the protection of the research centres in the Third World countries. Protestors in Nairobi had yesterday burnt down the Superseed research centre there, just when it was making a big contribution to research into the Superbug's possible predators. Government troops had fired on the demonstrators, making matters worse, and there had been such a small presence there of the Patents Police that disaster for the centre had become inevitable. Why, he asked, were the PP always reserved for the protection of Western centres and so rarely for use in Third World countries? The political officer replied by pointing out that there were just as many protesters gathering round the

Superseed European HQ here in Cambridge as anywhere else in the world. Jonas dryly suggested that they were a special target because this remained the intellectual headquarters of Superseed, even more than their American base in Detroit. Someone else said they couldn't understand why people should protest at the very centres where a scientific solution was most likely to be found. And Kassy, because she was involved in following the discussion, found herself saying firmly:

'But what if the solution is not a scientific one?'

A sudden silence fell right down the table, and everyone looked at her. Why had she opened herself up to another humiliation? She forced herself to stand up, very conscious that she was one of the youngest present.

'Well, we were asked for our lateral thoughts, so here goes…'

The silence deepened. What were they expecting?

'In our seed banks there are thousands of varieties stored. It costs a great deal of time and money to test them all for viability, so why not match them with suitable climates and give them back to the farmers and encourage them to grow any other heirloom varieties they may have stored. Somewhere there may be an answer hidden.'

The rights director was the first to recover. 'We've spent half a century discouraging farmers from planting anything but Superseed varieties. What about patent laws?'

'Could we not suspend them?' she said; but somebody laughed and Kassy, beginning to feel out of her depth, added tentatively, '… just for a while?'

'But what's in it for Superseed?' asked someone from sales.

'I'm sorry,' said Kassy, confused for a moment, 'I thought the problem was starvation, not how to protect our profit.'

There was a long silence round the table.

At length her father intervened softly. He sounded embarrassed by her, but determined to be patient. 'Well, this company is not a charity. Are you seriously suggesting that we give away our seeds for free to the rest of the world?'

'They were given to us for free in the first place –'

'Don't bandy history with me.' Though he laughed, Jonas's reply was swift. His scientific training had been limited, but he prided himself as a keen amateur historian. But then he relaxed and spoke more gently. 'It seems you want to scatter wild varieties over the face of the earth. Rather putting back the clock, isn't it? Rather a counsel of despair?'

Kassy was silent, and Jonas went on.

'If we try to put ourselves out of business, that's hardly going to help the hunger in the Third World. Quite the contrary. Transportation, roads, storage facilities, grain seed, markets, loans; the poor of the world depend on us for everything.'

Kassy sat down, defeated.

'I'm sorry, you asked for –'

'Quite. Do we have any other ideas?'

Jonas was ready to wind up the meeting.

'Then I can only urge the scientists to redouble their efforts. Look among the oldest seeds by all means, Kassy, for likely genes. I want all of you to try every technique you know. You're all aware of the urgency of the problem. But I've no doubt the answer will come from our best scientists as it always has. Somewhere out there, there's a Joe Goodman waiting. Perhaps it's worth putting before us as an inspiration Joe Goodman, the first discoverer and inventor of the original

Superseed, nearly sixty years ago; Nobel Prize winner and one of the great scientists of all time. There's just one little story about him that I'd like to tell you…'

Kassy could tell her father was trying to defuse the tension in the room.

'There's a story that after Joe Goodman invented the original Superseed he locked away his research where no one could find it, and disappeared for a couple of weeks, before he finally released it to the world. Nobody knows why he did it – one can't imagine it happening nowadays – but it's often said: What would have happened to our world today if there'd been an accident and everything had been lost? So go and tell your scientists, Jim, don't hide your research!'

There was laughter around the table, and over the top of it he cried, 'Just don't try it… the situation is too urgent. Let's have your research! And let's have it quickly!' Then he murmured, 'Thank you, the meeting's over,' and everybody was standing and gathering their papers.

Kassy was now conscious that most of the members of the board were avoiding her with their eyes. The boss's daughter was obviously an embarrassment. She started to slip out, feeling confused and angry all over again. Another failure, she thought.

In the corridor outside the meeting room, dusty rain was lashing the windows, and the sky outside was dark. It was one of those very brief but violent storms that sometimes punctuated the otherwise endless days of heat. Kassy put her head against the streaming window-pane, as Timothy came up beside her.

'Well you didn't help,' she said.

'I'm not sure if I agreed with what you were suggesting.'

'Get lost then.'

'Honestly, Kassy, it was rather naïve.'

He paused for a moment and then left, as she continued to stare down at the city. That rare burst of rain had stopped, and the ground was steaming.

Her father was one of the last to come out of the meeting. He looked at her for a moment and smiled.

'Come and have a bite to eat with me, Kassy. In about half an hour? It's a long time since we had a chat.'

'All right Dad,' she said. 'Thanks.'

She knew he meant it nicely, but her heart sank.

A 'bite' with Daddy, in his private suite in the penthouse, could be a rather embarrassing affair; it implied a three-course meal, served by one of those Indian servants who were becoming fashionable again among the very rich. They were a symbol of concern for Third World unemployment.

Her father passed her a glass of wine when she arrived.

'How's my rebel daughter?' he said, smiling.

'Fine,' she said, smiling back. No use complaining of back pain.

'This is only a Superstores common-or-garden wine,' he went on, 'but it's rather good, don't you think? Chinese Chardonnay. You won't mind if I just finish watching the news.' He indicated his desktop screen in an alcove of the room. 'Then I promise to put it out of my mind.'

He had swivelled the screen round to watch, and was standing now in the middle of the room, while she sat on the cream Chesterfield, trying not to let her eye be distracted by the rapid cutting of video shots from round the world. There were empty storehouses, the drawn faces of suffering peasants, the devastated fields swarming with insects. She tried to fix her eyes on the framed paintings on the alcove wall behind the huge desk. They were portraits of various chief executives, or eminent scientists, bigwigs from the past. But the images on the screen were demanding. She turned and looked down the room, at the deep, opulent chairs, the antique mahogany table, and through the great glass doors which looked out on to the wide tarmac roof of Superseed House. The storm had passed and she could just glimpse the shining tail rotor of Jonas's grey-green helicopter waiting on its pad, to take her father at a moment's notice, anywhere in Europe that he needed to be.

'Here's the really bad bit,' said Jonas and she was compelled to watch the screen again. 'Riots.'

Cairo seemed to occupy the most attention today; much of the centre of the city seemed to be on fire. There were further pictures of rioting in Delhi. She noticed the Indian servant falter as he passed on his way to lay the table, drawn for an instant to the news on the screen. Then there were shots of the new Superseed Centre in Beijing surrounded by crowds; and silent demonstrators with angry faces in Red Square. Suddenly the newscaster was signing off, and Jonas turned to Kassy with a weary look.

'Well we can't worry about it all the time,' he said and switched off. 'Let's sit down and have something to eat.'

The table was set for two.

'Nice to have my little girl to supper sometimes. These last few months just seem to have been one crisis after another, and I'm sorry if we haven't had so much time for each other.'

What does he want, she thought?

'How's the boyfriend?'

'Oh Dad, I told you, we broke up weeks ago.'

'Oh yes? Was it your fault or his?'

Did he really have to stir the pain when he wasn't very interested?

'It was by mutual agreement.' Very convenient thing to say. She remembered Timothy in tears, pleading with her to live with him, how much she'd despised him for it and then hated herself as much.

'Well I don't know. You're very choosy. Surely there's some nice young man –'

'Why do parents always want some nice young man?'

'Perhaps you'll never get married.'

Touché. 'Perhaps not.'

'Shame.'

'Why?'

'You need some support in life, littl'un. Your mother was a wonderful support to me before she died.'

She was more than that, Kassy thought. She was a slave.

'Dad,' she said, 'do we have to talk about this?'

'No,' he said vaguely, 'not if you don't want to…' He winked. 'Still Daddy's little girl then?'

She hated him at that moment more than she could ever have expressed in words. What made him so violent and vicious to her? It seemed to her that his own life had been sacrificed to climbing the ladder of success, making those who submitted to him feel small, not only in business, but even among his family and friends. A lonely man at heart, why should he so consistently prod at her loneliness?

'How's your brother?' he said.

Your brother, she thought; why not 'my son'?

'Boff? He's fine. Deep into his brain scans. He's got some wonderful new ideas about time and dreams, and how to visualise them effectively on computer screens. He believes the technology's there now to make some real breakthroughs.' She felt a sudden flush of enthusiasm and wanted to tell her father about Boff's ideas. 'He has this theory about dreams…'

'Theories. Dreams. He won't ever amount to anything.'

Kassy felt defensive of her younger brother. She sought for a way to engage her father's interest. 'Well, it could have quite an important commercial application.'

'How?'

'Well, for psychiatrists for instance. If you could play back people's dreams to them accurately, you could help their work a great deal.'

'Oh really.' Her father didn't seem convinced. 'Why doesn't he get a decent job. You'd think he could find something useful to do in a crisis like this.'

She knew Jonas deeply resented his son's failure. Two years ago, Boff had failed to join the corporation after his PhD. Kassy always felt Jonas really wanted his son to follow in his footsteps; instead it had 'only' been his daughter. Another disappointment for the old patriarch.

'Well,' she started, carefully, 'at the moment he doesn't want…'

'He doesn't want to settle down. He wants to pretend he's somebody without having to work for it.'

Kassy was stung by the injustice. 'He works very hard –'

'Pretending.'

She felt like saying 'so do you' but checked herself. Instead she said simply: 'I think he's somebody special.'

'Oh probably, very probably. All I know is, if he wasn't in a protected area, he couldn't behave the way he does.' The father dismissed his son. 'Let's talk about something else.'

The Indian bent over her. She hadn't been introduced, didn't even know his name. He was slightly plump with small feet and guarded, deep-set eyes.

Then Jonas was speaking again. He was blaming himself for being too touchy with her. 'I'm sorry if I seemed to put you down at the meeting this afternoon. I didn't really mean to. Your idea had some value and was certainly worth considering. But if you think it through, as I've done, I think you'll find it doesn't really work.'

'No, I know,' said Kassy. 'I just don't think we're holding enough viable seeds. And the original habitats in which they were developed have all gone.'

'But there'll be more money for viability testing. That's important work you know. You might have a gene or two in there that's of use to our scientists.'

'Yes,' said Kassy, trying not to appear dispirited, 'I had hoped so.'

'And anyway,' he added, as he attacked his beefburger with relish, 'your free-for-all is against the law. I've been checking with the lawyers.'

She stopped eating as he went on.

'No unauthorised seeds can be grown outside the laboratory or test sites. It applies to Europe and the US and now it's been adopted by all the significant members of the UN.' He laughed. 'I think there's only the deserts of Borneo left for you to try your seeds.'

After another mouthful, he added almost as an afterthought: 'I just wanted to warn you really, in the lightest possible way, not to think about trying any bright ideas on your own account, because it would be against the law. Not a good idea. Especially when your old Daddy's in charge of the corporation.' He smiled at her, but she always felt in some way threatened by her father.

'I wouldn't want my little girl picked up by the Patents Police, because there really wouldn't be much I could do. Except resign.'

He poured out the rest of the bottle into their glasses and changed the subject. The Indian's eyes met Kassy's for a moment as he took away the empty bottle, gripping it tightly in his small hands.

Everything seemed to reinforce her devastating sense of loss and failure. It hadn't really occurred to her before that she was looking after a massive library of seeds which could be poached for their parts in the lab, but never grown into plants in their own right out in a field. It was like an ancient garage full of beautiful vintage cars whose odd gearbox or carburettor might one day unexpectedly come in useful, but would never again be allowed to run on the open road. It surprised her that in two years in the job this minor point of legality had never occurred to her. It seemed to devalue her work yet again.

For the first time in her life she was beginning to dislike the idea of the Superseed. The God she had been brought up to worship was a jealous God, that would tolerate no rivals.

After dinner, they sat on the sofa for a little, with coffee, and watched part of quite a good nature programme on the new

41

ecology of the Amazonian scrublands. Afterwards Jonas rose and stretched, patting his distended stomach.

'Before you go,' he said, 'I must give you the latest volume of my history to read.' He strolled over to his desk to get a copy. He always called it 'my history' as if he had written it himself and not just commissioned it. She sometimes wondered if he'd have been a happier man as an historian than as a director of a corporation. He might have been a nicer man, at least.

'I'm ready to publish,' he said as he handed it to her, 'for the half-century celebrations, but I'm a bit worried about the timing.'

She glanced at it and could understand his reservations. *Superseed – The Golden Years* didn't seem a very apt title in the present crisis, half-century or not.

'Read it over the weekend,' he said almost shyly. 'Tell me what you think.'

'OK Dad,' she said.

'Well,' he yawned, 'it's been another long week. Are you off to the country?'

'Yes, first thing tomorrow,' she said.

'Well, take special care,' he said. 'These are difficult times.'

She hesitated.

'I was wondering if you'd lend me the car.' She felt suddenly sick for depending on him for such a rich life.

'Of course I will, littl'un. You can have it as much as you like at present; I'm not likely to get away. I'm glad you keep that place going. Your mother used to love it.'

'I know. Mind you, I'm not sure I do keep it going. It's getting very run down and overgrown.'

'Part of its charm, I daresay. But not for me.'

'You should come down one day, when you're less busy.'

'Oh, that'll be never,' he sighed.

'It's the only place left where I really feel at home,' she said quietly.

He stopped her on the way to the door.

'You're feeling a bit depressed, aren't you?'

Don't tell me what I'm feeling, her thought flashed back; but she said, 'A bit.'

'Is it the boyfriend or the job?'

'A bit of both.'

'Or this afternoon's meeting?'

'I don't really want to talk about it, Dad, if you don't mind.' I feel a complete failure, she thought, if you really want to know.

'Fair enough,' he said. 'Don't worry, have a quiet weekend. I've left the car in the usual place. Going on your own, are you?'

Thanks for that, she thought. 'Yes, Dad. Bye.'

As he watched his daughter go, Jonas was curiously moved by her. Beneath the prickly pride and fierce intelligence, she was so vulnerable, a little girl at heart. At the door he said casually: 'Goodbye, littl'un. Love you.'

He just caught the look of horror in her eyes as she closed the door.

Kassy walked home through the centre of the deserted city. It was a warm midsummer night, and the light was slowly fading from the sky above the shopfronts. Not that she usually worried overmuch about the dark. Cambridge was the administrative centre of Superseed, a protected scientific area; and with the Patents Police always in such numbers, it was now one of the

43

safest cities in the country. Yet when she heard the faint click of shoes on the pavement behind her, she was startled into alertness. It was as if someone was walking down the centre of the street behind her, measuring his footsteps with her own. It was a moment before she realised it was only the echo of her own feet from the shopfronts, and she relaxed again.

She passed Superfoods and Supermarks on the right and glimpsed the disused cinema on her left. Her anger and depression were still with her, and the word *failure* kept echoing through her brain. She noticed the new Superspud shop ahead with its gaudy advertisements for cheese fillings – 'Go for Geep'. It was closed early tonight. She turned automatically on the familiar way to King Street, till she could see ahead of her Danby's, the antique shop, above which was the flat she shared with Boff.

And then she had a sudden intuition. She had been so pre-occupied all her life by the comforting presence of Superseed, by her family and all their assumptions, by the successful cosy world of the scientists all around her. It was hard to think outside it all. And yet perhaps the answer would really be outside Superseed, in some other world completely. Thinking it through for herself was perhaps more important than her success, or her father's warnings, or even the law itself. She wasn't sure that she was thinking at all clearly yet. But she knew it was worth the effort. And for a moment, though afraid, she felt mysteriously better.

When she got home she stopped for a moment, and looked in at Danby's window, her eye caught by a lovely display of twentieth-century digital watches. Stopwatches, wristwatches and novelty watches all laid out together, some of them almost priceless, from the 1990s and even earlier. She could see a light on in the back of the shop; and Ginnie, old man Danby's daughter, was moving about making herself a cup of tea. Ginnie was a student at the university, and Kassie thought her brother might have been quite fond of her, if he wasn't so incapable of making any kind of approach to her.

Kassy let herself in, down the corridor between the shops and up the stairs. There Boff was stuck in front of the computer screen as usual. As she opened the front door of the flat she caught a glimpse of him in his room, wriggling in his swivel chair, like a baby excited by his food. He threw his long fingers at the keyboard, as if he was throwing a jelly on the floor.

'I just can't get this right,' he shouted at her in frustration, and ran his fingers through his thick curly hair.

She knew better than to interrupt and went through to her own room. She had shared this flat with her younger brother for three years now and on the whole they got on well together. He had such a childish one-track mind that he was rarely aware enough of human problems to be difficult. He cooked for them both occasionally and kept the kitchen clean, but most of the time he kept to his room at the back. It was piled from floor to ceiling. There were his computer screens and files and monitoring equipment and connecting equipment of all kinds that she didn't really understand. And there were boxes of recordings and metal cards, scientific journals and computer magazines. It was like a cross between a storeroom and a laboratory, and he was continually bringing in new equipment borrowed from the university – which officially he'd left after he'd got his PhD a year ago. Kassy didn't know how he funded his research now, but he seemed to collect quite a bit of equipment from Superseed. The centre of his operations was his desk and new personal computer, where he seemed to be almost permanently involved. Somewhere behind all the junk, in the dark recesses of his room, was his bed.

Her room, on the other hand, was at the front of the house, over the shop, as large as her brother's room but bare and open and sunny in the daytime. It was dominated by a large desk and a wide bed. It was tidy and cool and organised.

'Ah, that's better,' she heard from the other room. 'Now we're getting somewhere!'…

She went into the bathroom and then made some coffee in the kitchen. It was not real coffee like her father's but Supercaffin, made from 'genuine authorised coffee substitute' as it said on the tin. She could still hear Boff's explosive comments. She wondered, not for the first time, if he talked like this to himself when she wasn't there. He'd been sitting at that computer when she left for work that morning – in fact he'd been more or less in front of it for three days. And her father seemed to think he was lazy. She wondered what he was brewing up to.

'Now! Let's try this…'

Back in her room with her 'coffee' she suddenly felt very tired. She flicked on the screen and caught the last of the evening news. There was a Superseed spokesman defending the farming of kelp, but also stressing the importance of preserving life in the oceans. She changed the channels but switched off quickly. The desert and starving babies again. It was like a permanent backdrop to their lives.

'Yes! That's the one…!'

It was no use feeling guilty, she thought, it didn't help. She must do something. She stood helplessly and thought of getting to bed, but didn't seem to have any energy. What a day.

'Here, Kassy, come and look at this!'

She went through. Boff looked at the screen, fascinated. 'Here, let me show these whale-sound pictures first.' He slotted a metal card into his computer.

With an interdisciplinary degree in electronics, physics, maths and biology, Boff had specialised for his PhD in the translation of brainwave patterns into visual screen displays, a quite respectable broad area of research. The development of neural network computers had brought the study of the brain a long way since the early days of positron emission tomography. But the novel angle for Boff was in concentrating on whale sounds, the old recordings from the twentieth century. He had analysed them in various ways, and translated them from acoustic into visual images, and had begun to understand the way that whales conceived their thoughts. Lacking the evolutionary advantage of hands to develop the immediate practical intelligence of man, with all the attendant distractions of technology, their massive brains had developed instead along different lines. At first they had concentrated on space, mapping the oceans in amazing detail for the purposes of communication and mating. They had developed another area of their large brains for the purpose of mapping time, the history of their past and future, in a similar way. With their knowledge of time and space they had embarked on deeper thought, pressing for an understanding of their chances of survival, in a way barely comprehensible to man; projecting great slow archetypal images across the vast distances of the

47

ocean, in powerful and positive terms. Boff had planned a book about this for the general reader called *Whales – the Monks of the Sea* which hinted finally at the idea that the planet had been sustained by the prayer of whales, an idea so excessively outrageous that he went into paroxysms of glee whenever he described it to anyone. What he really loved was the idea that ninety-nine per cent of his book was meticulously researched and absolutely scientific; but it did seem to point to the real possibility of this conclusion, which he had intended to slip in over the last chapter or so, to really shock the scientific community. The problem was that, like most very rapid intellects, 'writing it all up' seemed rather boring.

There was also something of a problem in that whales were now extinct. Boff needed more material to work on, and his mind was forced to move on. He was drawn back to the study of man's mind: the connections between the visual cortex and the unconscious; its ability to operate, like the whales, in a region beyond space and time. He had also become fascinated by the possibility of singularities in space-time, where the normal day-to-day rules might be stretched or broken.

'Now look at this, Kassy,' he said, making way for her to sit in front of his screen. 'Last night I went back through my research and watched some whale visualisations. Now I was thinking about it a lot, went to bed and recorded my dreams.' He gestured towards a massive square kind of desk lamp in front of her. It was a more sophisticated version of the ultra-sonic dreamcorder that had enjoyed quite a craze among the general public in the early 40s.

'First look at this. A humpback whale, 1995, translated from the sounds.' He made a connection; and, from among the black heaps and dark piles of unconscious material at the far side of the room, a screen suddenly glowed into life. Sound-wave patterns were translated into beautiful mandala shapes, blues merging into greens, quadrilateral branching patterns of great beauty, unfolding with slow majesty. The very act of watching them seemed to give them a sense of meaning.

'Now try this.' He turned to the screen on his desk, next to the dreamcorder. Brainwaves were translated into a remark-ably similar pattern, though moving much more quickly. He played it back again, gradually slowing it down. At one point the two screens were almost identical and he stopped both screens. The resemblance was uncanny.

'No conscious control over this at all,' said Boff. 'Just my obsessional interest in the thought patterns of whales.' He grinned. 'Now, as the brain patterns slow, we're getting into a timeless area here, and then comes the possibility that we will be thinking the same thoughts together in a place beyond time. Now if our thoughts could merge at that point, it could cause a singularity in time. It is definitely theoretically possible, I've been doing the maths for it. I really think it's possible.'

He looked at Kassy, awestruck. He really did get dramatic, she thought. She was too tired to go on following this conversation for long. The idea of Boff merging thoughts with a long-extinct whale species seemed suddenly very farcical – if not to say unreal in comparison with the daily pictures of suffering on the television screens.

'Oh Boff,' she said, 'you've been working too hard, your brain's packing up.'

'Probably just the thing,' said Boff; 'bypass the conscious mind, give the unconscious a chance!'

'What would happen to you if you did cause a time singularity?'

'I don't know. Nobody knows. It's like the old atomic bomb. When people first had the idea over a hundred years ago, they thought it might cause a chain reaction to blow up the world. So I might collapse the whole of time into a different reality. Look.'

Boff suddenly ran off into the inner recesses of his room and, leaning over an old sofa somewhere, he suddenly emerged again grasping a long red balloon. Kassy was strangely taken aback, as if Boff were a magician, permanently entertaining at some party.

'Now just suppose,' said Boff, 'you were trapped in time on the inside of this balloon at one end. Here.' He pointed to one end of the balloon. 'But time-space might be folded over like this.' He folded the balloon over so that one end lay on top of the other. 'Now you are lying very close to something or someone else, in spite of the fact that you might be widely separated by time, or space for that matter.'

He really looks like a clown with that balloon, thought Kassy.

'Now what happens if you get through the skin of the balloon?' said Boff. 'You might collapse the whole of time into a different reality…' and the balloon exploded, shocking Kassy awake. 'Then you might disappear off the face of the earth,' said Boff, pulling a face. Kassy started to laugh. 'But on the other hand,' he said, 'you might get away with it. You might be merged into the mind of a twentieth-century whale.'

He swam floppily about the room a few times. She couldn't help laughing; he looked so lanky and spotty and not a bit like a whale. 'Or perhaps,' he went on, 'the whale would get in here.' He cowered back from the giant presence.

'You're absurd!' she said, glad to be able to be silly again.

'Who knows what would happen?' he said in mock horror. 'From the moment I merge with that poor whale's mind, every detail of life might change, from that moment to this. All the time in between might collapse into a different reality, might slip sideways from a mere potentiality into a different reality –' He was still clowning.

'What are you going to do next then?' said Kassy; and a wave of tiredness swept over her, so that she wished she hadn't asked the question. She crossed her arms on the desk in front of her, and laid her head on her arms.

But Boff was wide awake. 'Well I've got to stop using whales, I think. You see, everything in the calculations indicates that a singularity in time is only possible where as many factors as possible coincide.'

His voice seemed far away to Kassy. She hadn't realised how all the frustrations of the day had taken their toll on her.

'You've got to get together as many similarities of mood and place as possible. The same place, the same mood, perhaps some strong emotion, so that time becomes the only variable. That's the key…'

He sounded so awake to Kassy, leaping about, explaining.

'Well it's difficult to get to the Atlantic to be in the same place as a humpback whale and it's difficult to get calm enough to match a whale's mood…' He was fading out of sight to her, flailing his arms and laughing. She felt very, very tired.

'So I shall have to find a more oblique way of working.'

Surely she deserved to sleep now.

'Oblique…'
And so she slept.

The dream broke vividly into her mind.

She stood in the middle of a devastated field. Everywhere there were plants lying, pulled up, shrivelled, blighted. Burnt stubble. She felt very thirsty, but there was no water. Somewhere behind her she could see some tents, a well, the sound of happy laughter. She tried to turn back but she felt she would never get there. It was almost like a party, back there, with balloons and children's games. But she hadn't been invited and she had no strength to reach it. She needed water desperately and started to look about her. Where is the water, she thought, where are the whales? She started walking on. There were some dunes ahead of her, dried and cracked with the heat. Perhaps the water was over the other side. Suddenly she was on her hands and knees, crawling towards this sand dune.

And then she saw, crawling up the dune ahead of her on all fours, a newborn baby. It had the emaciated arms and legs and the distended stomach of the starving, and it crawled ahead of her on all fours, just as she herself was crawling. There were flies too, crawling all over the baby. The heat was oppressive, burning hotter by the minute. Then the flames burnt out, the baby was bursting into flame, it was turning black, the flies were burning too. It was shrivelling as it burned, turning. There was a crack in the earth nearby, like a hole. The blackening baby shrivelled and dropped into the hole in the earth.

She managed to get to the edge of the hole. She looked in. There was no baby left, just some black remains at the bottom of the hole.

Then she felt someone was coming up from behind her. Slowly she turned. A man was standing there. He looked at her for a long, long time, till time seemed to empty out all its meaning into a heavily charged space between them, till it seemed almost beyond time.

And then she woke.

Boff was standing over her, looking down.

'I'm sorry,' he said; 'did I startle you?'

'No,' she said, 'I had a dream.' She became aware suddenly of the warmth on her head, the big square dreamcorder like a bright desk-lamp poised over her head. She pushed it back, violently.

'You bastard,' she said. 'What have you been up to?'

'You don't mind do you?' He grinned at her. 'Hey, careful with that, it's a delicate instrument. Shall we go for it, it's on the computer?'

'Why the hell should you?' She had only just woken up and felt fierce. 'It's my dream.'

But he was already setting it up. 'Wouldn't you like to try it? Here.'

Despite herself she was fascinated. She knew the procedure, as she'd tried it before, but never when she could still remember the dream so clearly. By the time she'd been through it a couple of times with the dreamcorder reinforcing the images, it was misty but quite recognisable. Boff didn't seem to be able to read it as clearly as she did, but even he was impressed. Then they played it back again. Parts were shadowy: the party in the distance. There was something floating in the air that looked like shrivelled rubber.

'That's the party balloon,' said Boff. 'Obvious where that image came from!'

When it came to the burning baby, Kassy turned aside.

'You've been watching too much television,' said Boff.

Then a moment later: 'Who's he?'

He held the frame. To her it was the clearest image in the whole dream. Not an idealised or archetypal image, but a completely individual face. A period haircut, a brown jacket.

'I've no idea,' she said.

'Think,' he said. 'People in dreams are usually someone you've met, even if it's only very casually, passing in the street or something.'

She looked again at the face. For a long time. Suddenly it seemed almost as clear as a piece of film. His grey eyes looked back steadily, and seemed to be full of some question, to which she was expected to have an answer.

Boff went back to the start and played the whole dream again. Again he stopped at the face. In any case it was the end of the dream; the images fell apart after that. Where had she seen that face before? The longer she looked at it, the more compelling the face grew, the more urgent the question he seemed to be asking. But familiar though he was, as if she'd known him all her life, yet she couldn't be sure that she'd ever met this man before. She felt confused.

'Ooh, a secret boyfriend, eh?' said Boff, in a silly brotherly way. 'I wonder if he comes from the past or the future?'

'It's almost as if he wanted to know something,' she puzzled; 'something I can tell him.'

'Whether you're free on Friday night, perhaps?' said Boff.

Suddenly she felt furious.

54

She snatched the metal card out of the computer. 'Damn you!' she said. 'It's my dream. It's got nothing to do with you. What are you doing, putting my dreams on card? You can get on with your bloody research without using me.'

'Hey, Kassy –' Boff began, but she was in full swing now.

'Why don't you get a proper job. You're not a serious scientist at all.'

'Calm down –'

'You're a bastard and you can bloody well leave me out of it.'

And she threw down the card and went straight off to her room, slamming the door behind her.

She undressed quickly. She felt rather silly coming out again to go to the bathroom, so she banged about noisily with the taps and toothbrushes to show how furious she was. What a terrible day. Back in her room, she caught her reflection in the mirror for a moment, and sat on the end of her bed, weeping like a child at the helplessness of her life. Then she got into bed. The sooner the day ended, the better.

But as she drifted into a dark and dreamless sleep, it was as if she were sinking into deep, deep water.

She woke early at half past six, with her mind clear. Her first feeling was of anger, partly with Boff, but above all with her father. Both of them were so sure of themselves in their different ways and she felt so powerless: at a loss, all her instincts denied, cancelled out. Yet she was not a fool, she thought; surely seeds were never meant for one company's profit. Surely there must be some way to rediscover the diversity of the world's seeds. If the law had to be broken or changed, then so be it. She wanted to go to challenge her father, to confront him. But he would be busy, would not welcome a visit, would belittle her.

She tried to calm herself by reading, and she propped up a pillow on her bed and began to read the latest volume of the Superseed history which her father had given her. She started with the summary on the inside of the jacket.

This volume is the third part of the Superseed story.

The first volume – 'The Early Years' – deals with the establishment of the Superseed Empire 2000-2022. As the importance of military arms diminishes and energy supplies dwindle, the control of the world's food supplies becomes the dominant issue of the twenty-first century and the only secure future for a transnational company. Covers: the population explosion and the growing need for food; capture of the seed market by use of patent laws; alliance with the 'One World' environment movement; the building of the infrastructure, roads, storage etc to control high-tech food from seed to table.

The second volume – 'The Crisis Years' – deals with the blight of 2022-24 and the climate changes of the 20s and 30s. As much of the Third World becomes desert or is ruined by floods, the situation in Canada and Siberia improves. Super-seed is in the best position to benefit. Covers: Debt and the collapsing economies; death and the stabilising population; the mid-West dustbowl, drowning cities and Refugee Wars; Superseed to the rescue – the founding of the Patents Police; the clearing of the northern forests; worldwide control of water supplies and land use.

This, the third volume – 'The Golden Years' – deals with the period from 2038 to the present day. The great mono-cultures in Siberia, Canada and parts of Asia, come to dominate the world. Covers: The rise of the new internationalism; the

Patents Police and political stability; new breakthroughs in biotechnology; the 'Bread For All' programme and the spread of Food Aid to the very poorest...

Kassy flicked through the pages of the book and sampled the conclusions of the last chapter. Its triumphant tone was insulting; how could they publish this? No doubt her father would love to publish, and to add a brief personal epilogue, describing the crisis of 2047-50 and how the scientists had found an answer yet again, so everything was all right. No mention of how the very success of Superseed had made the world vulnerable to such a crisis in the first place. And not only this crisis, but others yet to come, to which scientists might have no possible answer, like the exhaustion of the over-exploited soil or collapse of water supplies. There was no hint of any of those issues in the book. She felt the anger and helplessness rising in her again.

She tried to cut off her feelings, and looked out of the window at the hazy blue sky. It was going to be the usual monotonous summer weekend with the temperature in the eighties. She left the book on the shelves behind her bed, got up and dressed and then made the coffee. But when she took a cup through to Boff's room, he wasn't there. She wasn't surprised; he often went in and out at the oddest times; sometimes he went off for walks in the middle of the night. She noticed the metal card she had flung down last night, still lying on the cluttered floor. She fed it into his PC and played it through again.

The man with the grey eyes looked at her out of the screen, intelligent, and concerned. Who was he, and how could she help him? The more she looked at him, the more disturbed she felt by it. She slipped it out of the computer and into her pocket. She wanted to consider it again some other time, when Boff wasn't there to laugh at her. But it was already eight o'clock and she had something else to do before she left for the country.

By nine o'clock she had walked to the labs. There were very few people around on a Saturday morning: only a familiar guard at the checkpoint outside, and the porter at reception. She took the keys and let herself into her office and through the security doors into the seed storage area. She went directly to get more samples of LV143 and several other likely seeds. She took them from their containers and rewrapped them carefully. With the seeds in her shoulder bag she walked out through security and back towards the town, to find her father's car. The little red car was parked in its usual place on the slope outside the newsagent's. She put her bag in the boot of the car and slipped into the driver's seat.

There was no scientific value in what she was going to do. Most of the seeds she was taking out were already under official field trial, without success. It was only a minor symbolic gesture. But she was following her own intuition, instead of the accepted clichés in her life, and her heart felt lighter for it. She felt no guilt that she was breaking the law, rejecting the company, disobeying her father. She even felt a secret pleasure that she was using his borrowed car to transport the stolen seeds.

She started the car and moved off down the slope, taking the familiar weekend route out of town, to her cottage in the country.

Chapter Three

'Hello?'

The telephone had startled him.

'Hello Joe, haven't you got up yet?'

Time seemed to have folded back on itself, and it took a moment for Joe to unfold it. He had a heavy head. He was at home, lying in bed, the telephone receiver in his hand.

'What time is it?'

'Nearly midday.'

Joe groaned.

'Oh, sorry!' The other end of the phone was apologising exaggeratedly. 'You've not got anyone there with you? Have you? Oh dear, I've not interrupted you have I? Is Sarah there?'

'Oh, shut up Tony. All I've got here is a headache. What do you want?'

'Are you going anywhere this weekend?'

'I haven't got any plans.'

'Can I pop round for a few minutes?'

Joe had a bath, made himself some real coffee, made the bed and tidied his room. Today he was not going to the labs for the first day in months. He had the weekend – till he gave in his research on Monday – and had no idea what to do with it. He felt utterly spare. He sat at the bare table in the window and stared at the tree across the road, waiting for Tony. Some child had stuck an Asterix poster in the window of the flat above the newsagent's. A bicycle went down the slope. He waited vacantly without a thought in his head. Then he noticed there was a curious little red car parked across the road which he didn't remember having seen before; it was an unusual two-seater design. But he thought no more about it.

There was a knock on the door downstairs. He ran down. It was Tony, in a light blue sports jacket. Very chic. Joe led him upstairs to his first-floor room. While Joe went into the kitchen to make some more coffee, Tony called through from the front room.

'When are you going to get a proper place of your own? This place looks like digs for an undergraduate.'

'Well, I've hardly been around lately.'

Joe came through with the coffee and they settled at the table by the window, and grinned at each other.

'Well, how does it feel to be famous?' said Tony. 'Tasted the fruits yet? You're such a dark horse – I'll bet you smuggled Sarah out the back door just before I arrived. Or was it Gilda? No, I have a feeling that you favoured Sarah, didn't you, you rampant passion-fiend.'

'I'm shattered,' Joe said, still grinning. 'I wouldn't be much use to either of them at the moment!'

'Forgotten how to do it, eh?'

'I don't get your practice,' said Joe.

Tony laughed, happy to be flattered.

'What are you after then?' said Joe at last.

'Nothing special,' said Tony. 'I just wondered if I could have a squint at your research this weekend before it goes to *Nature*. I'm dying to get the hang of it. Mac's given the OK.'

'When are you off to Cairo?'

'In a week or so. I want to lay the groundwork, get some field trials set up perhaps? So I need to understand what I'm selling; maybe even take a summary of your paper. Hot off the press. What do you think?'

'Well, you could, I suppose –'

'I can't wait,' said Tony gleefully, standing up.

' – but it's not here I'm afraid. I left it at the labs.'

'Jesus Christ, Joe, do you know what you're doing?' He sat down again slowly. 'Have you left a copy with Mac?'

'Oh no, that's a point. I'll do it on Monday.'

'Are you saying that the only copy is just lying around in the labs, Joe?' Tony had gone white. He sighed. 'We'd better go and get it.' He looked at his watch. 'I was driving Carol down to London this weekend, but I suppose... Have you photo-copied it?'

'No, but it's all right.'

'Joe, you don't know the dynamite you've got there. Suppose you lost it –'

'It's all in here,' said Joe, tapping his head. 'Anyway, it's really not as important as you're making out.'

'You're completely naïve, do you know that? You've got to get your research published, out in the open. What happens if another company publishes the idea first? You'd have ruined all our efforts. Lead times are everything. Speed is crucial.'

'Yes, I suppose so.' Joe suddenly felt depressed at Tony's vehemence. There had always been such pressure on him to produce the goods. He'd had enough of it.

'Shall we go and get it then?' said Tony.

'It really is safe,' said Joe. 'Under lock and key. I just can't face going over to the labs today. It's my first day off for months. Why don't you pop round on Monday. I'll give you a copy then.'

Tony looked very reluctant. 'OK,' he said, and sounded a bit hurt.

'Sorry,' said Joe. 'Morning after.'

Tony shrugged. 'OK,' he said.

There was a silence.

'The fact is,' said Joe, trying to be honest, 'now I've finished all this work, I don't know how much it's really worth.'

'What?' said Tony, incredulous.

'I don't know,' said Joe. 'I had a weird dream last night. Like a party gone sour.'

'Tell me,' said Tony, and put on his best listening look.

So Joe told him.

Then he said, 'It's as if I suddenly can't see the point of it all.'

'You must be crazy,' said Tony. 'Completely crazy. You've invented a seed which is going to save the Third World countries a fortune in fertilisers and pesticides and herbicides. They'll be able to produce more cash crops to sell back to us. That gives them lots of foreign currency to buy our goods and develop their economies. They become rich and can afford to feed their populations. The whole world economy benefits. Success on success on success! It's great! It's progress! What's got into you?'

'Well, it's not as if it's some kind of wonderseed for all time. There'll always be changing soils and mutating pests to deal with…'

'Great,' said Tony. 'A job for life. For both of us.'

As Tony became more enthusiastic, the energy seemed to drain out of Joe. 'It's just that…' He stopped and stared at the table in front of him.

'What?'

'There's something I can't… I wish…'

He ground to a halt, completely inarticulate.

For a moment Tony looked genuinely concerned. 'You've been working too hard,' he said gently. 'You were the same after finals, do you remember? You got so depressed and suddenly didn't see the point of it all. We spent all the time at that bloody pub by the river drowning our sorrows. And then you walked off with a first, and I got a pathetic two-two.' He laughed merrily. 'Sod your temperament. The price of genius, I suppose, but I'm damned if I'm paying too much attention.' He got up and stretched. 'Well, thanks for the coffee. I'll leave you to it now; I must go and collect Carol. I'll call round first thing on Monday morning, and we'll go to get your research together. You need looking after, that's your trouble. Keep cheerful. Got any plans?'

'Not really. A quiet day. Might go for a walk.'

'Don't mope about the flat. Give Sarah a ring. I know you've got her number because she told me. I reckon she could be quite keen on you. Unwind a bit.' He waggled his eyebrows up and down in mock suggestiveness, till Joe laughed.

'Yes I must,' said Joe.

'I think,' whispered Tony, 'she's after your Superseeds.'

Joe had just seen Tony out when his friend came back, and poked his head round the door again.

'Hey, did you hear my idea for an advertising slogan?' He paused for effect and then proclaimed: '*Nothing Succeeds Like Superseeds!*' He did a little dance, and grinned at Joe. 'Good, don't you think?'

Joe couldn't help smiling. 'Sod off,' he said.

Joe crossed to the window and watched his friend go into the newsagent's opposite. He stood musing for a moment. Then he noticed the little red car was still there, across the road. Like a message, waiting for someone. What a strange model it was. Custom-built probably. Very small and battered. He went over and sat in his armchair, and for a few minutes he stared at the dark television screen without a thought in his head. He wondered what he should do with himself, deprived of his work. Tony was right: it would take a few days or even weeks to unwind from the pressure he'd been under; he must expect some reaction. He was free now to do anything that came into his mind. Perhaps he'd ring this Sarah girl. But somehow he couldn't face the effort this morning. He stared at the dark screen in front of him and the images of his dream last night began to form in his mind. Collapsing balloons in a desert wilderness. A girl turning towards him. To keep out such thoughts, he turned on the television. Somebody was doing a manic comic routine. It was one of those marathon charity shows for the needy, all red noses and open generosity. The comedian was contorted in a parody of excessive passion, his loins thrust towards the audience. Joe wandered over to the window.

The little red car was still there.

Behind him he was aware that the television screen had gone into paroxysms of laughter and cheering. Joe felt strangely guilty. Surely he of all people had done enough to help the needy? Or had he? It had always been put to him that his discovery would help the Third World, help them to be less dependent. And yet, would it really help the poor...? He felt in a very strange state.

Suddenly a girl was crossing the road toward the car, with her back to him. All at once his concentration upon her was total. He knew with a shock, from the tilt of her neck and the curl of her fair hair, that it was the girl he had seen in his lab the night before, the girl of whom he had dreamt. If this was a trick of the imagination, it seemed surprisingly real now. What was she doing outside his house? Was she some kind of journalist or industrial spy? It would have been easy enough to walk into the labs, he supposed. But that she was now in the street outside his home was surely unlikely to be a coincidence. He watched her open the boot and put a shoulder-bag in the back. She looked around to see if she were being watched, and instinctively he stepped back from the window. Then she was getting into the car, starting it up.

The immediacy of his own response even took him by surprise. One moment he was casually turning off the television, the next he was halfway down the stairs of the cottage. Checking he had his keys as he ran, he pulled the front door to behind him and ran to his Renault 5 which was parked just outside the house facing down the slope. The red car was just moving off ahead of him. He got into his own car, started up and pulled away from the kerb. And then suddenly, as he glanced ahead again, he realised with a shock that the red car he was following had quite simply vanished into thin air.

The shock struck him so powerfully that he jammed on the brakes and stopped with a dreadful jolt. He sat there bewildered. There was nowhere it could have gone. There were no turnings before the main road at the bottom of the little hill.

Cautiously, full of self-doubt, he moved forward again. The car nearly stalled, so he accelerated and the car now shot forward down the hill towards the main road. Instinctively he indicated towards the city centre. But glancing the other way, he saw the red car only a few yards away moving off in the opposite direction. Again it seemed to have appeared out of nowhere. Quickly he turned after it, in some confusion about what was happening to him, but determined not to let the red car out of his sight again.

Coming out of the newsagent's with some of his favourite small cigars, Tony was just coming to the conclusion that nothing would prise Joe away from his rooms that weekend; he seemed as stuck as a mollusc on a rock. In spite of all his jokes, Tony was beginning to worry about Joe. He could sometimes be a bit obsessive, but never so strangely incoherent. He glanced up at Joe's first-floor windows, just in time to see Joe fling himself out of the cottage, slamming the front door; leap into his car; start off fast; stop dead; start again slowly; race for the main road, indicate one way and then shoot off in the other; and then disappear from sight; all for no apparent reason.

And strongly into Tony's mind came a question about Joe's balance of mind. He stood on the kerb for a long time, considering what he should do about it.

*

Kassy drove mechanically along the familiar weekend route, driving slightly too fast around the corners, knowing that the chance of meeting other traffic on these roads on a Saturday was extremely slight. Only the very rich could afford the taxes on private cars, let alone the fuel costs. Already the heat was building up, and she opened the side windows. It was going to be another of those relentless days with the greenhouse haze high above shutting in the heat.

After a few minutes she came to a series of signs: YOU ARE LEAVING THE SUPERSEED SECURITY AREA.

She could already see ahead the huge red advertising balloon with its golden lettering that had been recently launched by Superseed as part of the fiftieth anniversary celebrations and which now floated above the North Checkpoint.

Not long after, she could see the high perimeter fence, and slowed to the checkpoint itself. There she showed her ID pass to the green-uniformed policeman at the barrier. She realised with a shock that there were a much greater number of green uniforms in evidence today, leaning in lazy groups against the sunny guardhouse wall, or standing in the shade cast by the huge balloon. Usually these checkpoints were very lightly manned: just a quiet reminder of where the demarcation of authority lay between the Patents Police and the national force.

The guard on the barrier knew her, of course, and knew the little red car.

'Morning, Miss,' he smiled.

'What's up today?' she asked him.

'Routine training exercise,' he answered flatly. She knew at once he'd been told to say that. 'Drive carefully.'

She filled up with Alcol at the Superseed station just beyond the checkpoint. Best Siberian had gone up again; the crisis seemed to be affecting everything. She collected some of her rations there, wondering how anyone could manage at all with food at such a price. Then she paid for the toll road. It was still the quickest way to get to the cottage. Once out on the toll road, she felt the familiar lifting of the spirits as she left Cambridge behind her. The long, straight road was almost empty; she only passed one Superseed truck on its way from some distant farmland. She steered between the occasional weed-filled cracks with the skill of the experienced traveller. Her father had owned this little car for over twenty years and it still ran well. It had been built to last, in the best and most expensive traditions of the twenties. If it had a problem it was the suspension, and Kassy had a nasty suspicion that this was her fault for driving too fast. The car also had a little sunroof, because it had been built before the scare of '29, and now she slid it back, jamming on her old yellow hat as a precaution, and felt the breeze in her face.

On either side of the road stretched the long fields of summer wheat, hardly divided into fields at all, mostly without hedgerows or dividing trees; stretching from the very edge of the road, right away to the most distant horizon where a line of windmills masked the edge of sight. At this stage of the season the wheat looked deceptively promising.

Soon she could see ahead, at the top of a long slow rise, the familiar old billboard she loved, which had been there as long as she could remember. It brought back her childhood in the 20s as nothing else could. She would ride in the car beside her mother, Boff on her knee, or later in the back seat; her father always too busy to come with them. Her mother would lift her hand from the wheel and point it out excitedly, every time as if it were a new discovery.

'Look, Kassy, look. There's the Superseed sign.'

It had always looked very old and battered, but it was a landmark in the long identical miles of wheat. It would look both ways, so you could see it on the way to the cottage, or on the way back. It read, in big letters:

GIVE US THIS DAY OUR DAILY BREAD

Then there was a picture of a huge loaf of bread, and on it was written the word 'Superseed'. And then underneath it said:

SUPERSEED ANSWERS THE PRAYERS OF THE WORLD

And there it stood, a battered billboard, in a wide sea of growing wheat. And she loved it, as she could never imagine loving the gaudy new advertising balloon at the North Checkpoint. 'Good for Daddy!' she would cry and clap her hands. It was almost like a ritual. After all, her Daddy *was* Superseed: he seemed to practically own the company, at least the European end. It almost made him out to be a god, which seemed no surprise to a five-year-old girl. And besides, what finer ambition could there be, than to be in a position to bring bread to the world? That ideal had sustained her through university and when she had trained in Montreal, through her months in the wheat fields of Siberia, and when she had come back to rejoin her father at headquarters. It was only this present crisis that had made her question at all. But now the poor were starving as never before and the gods had feet of clay. She was torn between guilt and anger, her deepest instincts were at war, and only at the cottage could she forget it, and be quietly herself for the weekend, without pressure.

She fell to musing, coasting along, enjoying the slight breeze which relieved the heat of the sun. A dark green van passed. Over on her left, a plume of smoke was rising above the fields. She wondered if there was a fire. Then from somewhere in the distance came a crackle like automatic laser fire. Probably a shooting range. Or that police training exercise perhaps.

There was no other traffic on the road now. There were never many trucks anyway on a Saturday, so that she had almost got out of the habit of using her back mirror.

But something made her glance up for a second, and notice an extraordinary thing. Behind her, as if hoping to overtake, she glimpsed for a moment another private car, of a strange shape, older than vintage, almost like a car from the previous century. She slowed down, and thought she could see a man driving, but she couldn't see his face clearly. For some reason his windscreen wipers were moving. The sight was almost comic.

Suddenly her car hit a slight tuft of grass on the road. She turned abruptly to the front again, to concentrate on the road ahead, and when she looked back later the car seemed to have gone. It was strange; perhaps some joyrider in a custom-built copy of an antique. But then she thought no more about it. She had been driving for nearly fifteen minutes out of Cambridge; and over the next rise, and the bend in the road, was her favourite sight.

As she came up over the crest, and the road dropped away, there it was. Across the wide horizon, like a smile, lay the distant line of deep blue which marked the Cambridge Sea. In the car and all around her she could taste the slight tang of the salt air. The smell of childhood weekends by the sea, when life was innocent and fun. The smell of freedom.

*

Joe had trouble keeping the strange car in his sight. He lost it from view once or twice, in busy traffic; but once on the dual carriageway, it was a little easier. It began to rain, a downpour so heavy that he could hardly see through the windscreen. Yet, after a time, he thought he saw her yellow blinking lights indicating to the left. Hopefully he took the next turning, signposted to a village he didn't know at all. He followed the road over the dual carriageway, past a small farm and an orchard, a village pub and a parish church. The rain had stopped now. Ahead, he could see the wide green fenland stretching to the horizon, dappled and patched with cloud. His heart rose for no reason, except that he was glad to have been drawn into the countryside. He wound down the window. The smell of the earth after rain. The smell of freedom.

Then he glimpsed a cottage ahead, on his right between some trees, and suddenly there was the red car slowly sliding out of sight around the back of it. He had tracked her to her destination.

He tried to think quickly. There was a short driveway to the cottage, overgrown with ancient trees. At the entrance, leaning into the road, was an ancient sign: 'FOR SALE OR TO LET', with the name of a Cambridge estate agent's. It occurred to him that he could pretend to be a prospective purchaser. Boldly, he drove straight into the driveway. He bumped slowly down a deeply grooved track, worries about his car's suspension nudging his mind, as wet branches scraped and stroked the side of the car. He came to a halt in front of a beautiful Victorian cottage, overgrown with wisteria.

He wondered whether he should knock on the old wooden door; but he had seen the red car slip round the side of the house only a few seconds earlier, so he decided to leave his own where it was and walk round to intercept her. He tried to work out what he would say to the girl. Could he ask her about her presence in the laboratories? And why she had parked outside his house?

There was a poplar tree growing at the corner of the house. Beyond it, as he turned the corner, he imagined he would see the back garden, cultivated perhaps with a little lawn, a rose arch, and a greenhouse in the background. Perhaps she had heard him drive in and she would be there, leaning against the car, waiting for him, ready with all the answers for him. He felt strangely moved, as if what lay around the corner were very important. As if the answers would be more significant than he yet knew. He was aware for a moment of an intense silence. The silence of expectation.

And yet when he turned the corner and came round to the back of the house, there was nothing. Quite contrary to his expectation, there was no red car parked there at all. No girl.

Just an old disused paddock overgrown with tall grasses and weeds, and surrounded by trees. He stood there stunned by the empty wildness of it. There was only the deep stillness of the afternoon, the buzz of a few insects and the sound of occasional raindrops splashing heavily from the surrounding trees. No sign that the red car had ever been there.

Had he been following a mirage? He didn't understand what he was doing there in the middle of the countryside, nor what had led him there. He felt confused.

Again, it was time for him to go home.

*

Kassy had been wondering about that strange old car she had seen behind her. Just before she got to the cottage, she thought she saw it again, following her. Private cars usually belonged only to senior Superseed staff. Otherwise there were only Superseed lorries on the roads, or the dark green vans of the Patents Police.

She drove back down the drive between the old fruit bushes, and round the back of the cottage where she usually parked, by the little lawn and the rose arch. She got out of the car, and leaned against the warm bonnet, waiting, half expecting the noise of a car following her down the cottage drive. A wave of fear came over her as she remembered the seeds she held illegally in the boot of her car. Perhaps the plain-clothes men had come to question her. She waited, tense with expectation.

At that moment, she heard the heavy sound of a helicopter and, looking up, saw it approaching like a giant insect, the letters PP standing out in black on its green body. A helicopter was a rare sight here. It must mean that the Patents Police were out in force, looking for trouble all around the Cambridge area. Yet somehow, as it thundered away again, that helicopter broke the spell for her. Surely it could mean nothing personal. It was, in any event, extremely unlikely that the police would follow her here; she was protected by the complete position of trust her father held. One day, perhaps, her father might come, but he was an administrator with a background in history and business studies. He had no detailed knowledge of biology, or the natural sciences, so that she could grow illegal plants in front of his nose and he'd never know the difference.

Taking courage again, she walked decisively round to the front of the cottage. There was nothing there. No car. The sun was quietly warming the grapes on the front wall. Perhaps she was becoming paranoid.

She returned to the back of the cottage, opened the boot of her car and took the envelopes containing the seeds from her shoulder-bag. She took them through the rose arch and into the little well-dug field beyond.

As she sorted the envelopes she looked across the field with dismay. These were not the first seeds she had taken from her own Superseed base collection to try to grow in the back garden of her cottage, though she had not then known it was illegal. She had been experimenting for some weeks in a less serious way; in fact since early spring. But now the failure had more meaning for her. Another week had brought no change. Not a single green shoot had raised itself above ground. There was sterility from end to end of the garden. Her heart sank. She was already streaming with sweat in the hot sun, and she longed to go into the cool cottage, have a shower and change, pour herself a drink. But instead she tried to still the anger and pain in herself by quietly raking over the ground, preparing drills, marking the rows and half rows, sowing the precious seeds. Even if these experiments failed, no one could say she had not tried, and no law or loyalty to company or family would stop her.

But, she felt, if she continued to fail, where could she turn for help?

Chapter Four

When Joe got back to his flat in Cambridge, there was a message waiting for him on the answerphone. It was from Mac.

'Joe, I'm in my office this morning. Could you drop by? Bring your research.' Joe suddenly felt desperate to escape, to turn round and drive straight back to the country, or anywhere else. He wondered who he could turn to. He badly needed to take stock. The last thing he wanted to do was to talk to Mac.

But he knew there was no escape. He decided to get it over with, and set out straight away. Yet the curious thing was that, whereas he had meant to go by way of the labs, to collect his research, in fact he next became aware of himself standing outside an estate agent's in the middle of town.

There in the window was a picture of the cottage from the road, with its sign 'For Sale or To Let' standing upright in the foreground. Joe wondered if the girl might live there, so he went in to make enquiries.

The young estate agent inside quickly found the details.

'Some scope for modernisation there sir, I should say. But that's reflected in the very reasonable asking price.' The man, who was very young, seemed to relish speaking the clichés.

Joe soon discovered that the owner had died some time ago and had left instructions that the cottage should be sold and the money divided. 'To be honest with you sir, we're having a little trouble moving the property; it's a bit out of the way, so we're also prepared to consider short lets, until we can find a buyer, just to keep the place warm, as it were…'

'Is there anybody else interested at the moment?' Joe asked.

'To be honest with you sir, not at this moment in time.' The man looked unhappy.

Any idea that the girl might be a prospective buyer evaporated. Joe puzzled about the girl's connection with the place.

'I'm sure the property will begin to attract a lot of interest now that the market is picking up again,' the estate agent was going on hopefully. 'It's a very desirable residence with a wealth of original features. To be honest with you sir, a snip at the price.'

There was one last possibility, Joe thought, and he made roundabout enquiries about the man's colleagues. But it was soon clear that there were no girls working for the agency at present. The girl was neither buyer, seller, nor agent; and Joe had reached a dead end. The curious thing was, he hadn't really expected anything else. He expressed great interest in renting the property, with a view to possible purchase, and beat a retreat with the details stuffed into his pocket, and a promise to get in touch.

Joe walked on to see Mac. The PCCI building was a small anonymous block of offices in the streets behind Parkside, and he took the lift to the fifth floor. McAndrew was walking about his tidy modern office, waiting for him.

'Ah Joe,' he said, extending his hand. 'Good of you to come. It's nearly lunchtime. Have a drink?' He pointed to a glass-fronted cabinet. 'Whisky?'

'No, thanks,' said Joe warily. Mac could be deceptively sharp and Joe's head was still a little heavy from the night before.

'Great party last night,' said Mac, reading his mind. 'Congratulations. Sit down. I left a bit early I'm afraid. I always feel a bit exhausted surrounded by all those exceptional people. I don't know where you all get your energy. I really think I'm quite happy to be a dull old businessman. Middle age is coming to terms with your limitations. Brought me a copy of your research, have you?'

'Oh, no. I forgot. I'm sorry, I'll bring it in on Monday.'

'Ah, I see.' There was an edge to Mac's voice. He straightened his tie, and then ran his finger around his collar. 'So long as it's safe.'

'Oh yes, locked up safe.' Joe was getting a bit sick of all this.

'Mm. Well, all right then. Bring it in first thing Monday. Don't be late. And you're feeling all right are you?'

'Yes, fine.'

'Obviously you'll have a bit of time now to follow up the field trials in more detail –'

'And there are a few loose ends I want to pursue –'

'Of course. But it would probably do you good to have a bit of a holiday. What do you think?'

'Well, yes, I wouldn't mind a break for a week or two. I was thinking –'

'Good idea. Very good idea!' said Mac with unexpected vehemence. Then he looked out of the window over the nearby roofs, and pulled at his collar again. 'You must be feeling pretty tired. Pretty exhausted.'

'Yes.' Joe began to be a bit suspicious. Mac never said things like that without a reason.

Then Mac repeated himself, playing with the words. 'Pretty exhausted…'

'Why do you say that?'

'Well, it's only natural after such a long time under pressure.'

'Yes?'

'Yes of course.'

'What have people been saying?'

'Well, I'll be frank with you,' said Mac. 'There's no pulling the wool over your eyes. We're all a bit worried about you. You've been working too hard for some time. And it's in our interests to look after you. You know me. I don't believe in the heavy-handed approach. Plenty of freedom for my scientists. That's the way to get the best results…'

Joe rapidly lost interest in listening to Mac's soft Scottish speech and found himself watching the office door, which had been left ajar. One or two people were passing on errands from one office to another. But then, quite suddenly, Joe caught a glimpse of curly fair hair and a black dress passing by. It was only the briefest glimpse but it was unmistakably her. Instinctively he leapt up from his chair, and saying 'Excuse me for a moment' he rushed into the corridor.

She had rounded the corner and he raced after her. She was there; down the further end of the corridor already, walking quickly away from him. His heart pounded as he ran after her, bumping into a suited figure who emerged from an office unexpectedly. He finally caught up with her at the far end, as she slipped into the tea bar. He stretched out a hand to touch her arm. But how could he approach her, what could he say?

'Excuse me,' he said.

She stopped and turned slowly to face him.

'Yes?' she said.

He stopped, thunderstruck, as she looked at him. Then she laughed and slipped behind the counter. It was not the girl he had expected at all. He already knew this girl with the cheerful lopsided smile.

'Tea or coffee?' she said.

'Er... Two teas,' he replied. She served behind the tea bar here on a Saturday morning. Had she noticed his strange behaviour? What did she make of it? Yes of course she had noticed it, and clearly thought he was mad. Now he could see, her hair wasn't even remotely the same. What was happening to him? He felt a sense of excruciating embarrassment as he made his way back down the corridor, with two teas in plastic containers. He didn't know how to face the next moment either.

He didn't dare look up as he came back into Mac's office.

'Er... I thought you might like a cup of tea,' he said, putting one of the plastic cups down on Mac's desk. He kept the other one and sat down. He was painfully aware that he had rushed out in the middle of one of Mac's developing speeches. He tried to pretend it was all quite normal. He took a sip, and then looked up, as casually as he could.

Mac was looking at him with amazement and horror. His voice was full of concern.

'Is there anything you want to talk over with me?'

'Er… No, I don't think so. I'm quite happy.'

'If you really want to know, it's Tony who's been worried about you, and I can see why. He said you were having doubts about things. Talking about your dreams. Driving erratically. We don't want to lose you in an accident…'

'Did you say Tony?'

'I want you to take a holiday. Get that research to me personally first thing on Monday, and we'll get it straight to the publishers, announce it to the press. Then I want you to take at least two weeks. Go and lie on a beach somewhere. The Caribbean perhaps. I've always fancied the Bahamas myself. But tell me where you go, so we can keep in touch. Have you any ideas?'

'No,' Joe lied, 'but I'll let you know.'

'Do that. I also want you to go and see the doctor. Just a check-up. No time like the present.'

He straightened his tie, and reached for the phone.

The company doctor was in his surgery. Not an old man, he nevertheless looked worn out as if he'd been on duty far too long; but he'd obviously been told to check over Joe as a matter of priority. He shambled about doing all the usual tests, but he could find nothing much physically wrong, and so he advised immediate holiday with plenty of physical exercise.

'You've been living in your head for far too long,' he said. 'I expect mental exhaustion is at the root of your problem.' And he looked at Joe reassuringly. Joe couldn't help noticing the deep rims under his sagging eyes. 'If you catch yourself behaving strangely at all, then this is the man to see.' He handed Joe a card. 'Our resident psychologist, you know. But I don't really expect there's any need for it. Look after yourself.'

As Joe left he wondered whether he should have told the doctor about this girl he kept seeing, but decided it would sound either quite ridiculous or far too important. He glanced at the name on the card. Of course, it was Ivan Davitsky. He already had his card from the party. Might be fun to carry on their talk about synchronicity some time.

Walking back across town, he felt lighthearted again. All this concern for him was rather absurd, but he'd take their advice and have a holiday. He looked back in at the estate agent's. The young man was still there. Before he knew it, he was writing out a cheque for a month's rent, and a map and the keys to the cottage were in his pocket.

At the door, he turned back.

'I've been advised to take physical exercise. Would there be any objection to doing a bit of work in the garden?'

'Of course not, sir,' smiled the young man sycophantically. 'If you want to grow any flowers, or suchlike. As a possible future owner, I'm sure you'll be careful.'

Joe then went home, taking the keys to the cottage. He planned to go there on Monday morning after he'd handed in his research. He spent the rest of the day quietly at home. It rained heavily in the afternoon, a soft summer rain. He watched an old film on television – it was Hitchcock's *North by Northwest* – and he tried not to think too much. In the evening he cooked himself something to eat, hamburgers and some vegetables, though he didn't feel very hungry. Then he went early to bed, feeling exhausted.

He woke in the middle of the night with an acute sense of danger, which he couldn't explain to himself. Something to do with his work. How could it be dangerous? He tried to think if he'd been dreaming. Slowly and dimly something came back to him. In his dream he'd been laying landmines in no man's land. He'd wanted to desert, but knew that if he did, he'd be shot. He lay, staring at the ceiling for a moment. The dream had slipped away now. He wished he could talk to somebody about his work. The meaning of his work. With Jilly, he could never talk about his work at all. With Marie-Claire and Jimbo he could never talk about anything else but its technicalities. With Tony he had tried, but failed; and somehow he didn't quite trust him, especially now. Yet he felt a great unexpressed need to understand his work, its meaning for the future, where it was leading. He only knew there was something wrong. If only he could see into the future...

He lay awake with the common paranoia of loneliness battering in on him. The vision of this girl in the lab, in the red car, kept recurring to him; it was unreal. He'd always been accused of being slightly obsessive. In his work it had seemed an advantage. But was he transferring his obsession for his work to this girl? Perhaps he was really ill. He felt the strong desire to escape, to find space where he could sort himself out; somewhere where people weren't forever looking at him, judging him.

So, after a restless night, he got up very early on Sunday morning and quickly packed a suitcase, took sheets and some provisions, packed up the car, and drove off to his new cottage as fast as he could get away. And as he left Cambridge and came up on to the dual carriageway in the fresh light of dawn, he felt suddenly released. The sun was rising behind him and the early Sunday morning road lay flat and straight and empty ahead of him. He was leaving everything behind him, and no one in the world knew where he had gone.

The cottage was beautiful. It was furnished sparsely. It was old but dry, and there were blankets on the bed. There were only two bedrooms; the main bedroom looked out over the back garden, while the other spare room was little more than a box-room, now quite empty. The living room downstairs also looked out over the back garden and had a sofa and a chair. The kitchen ran down the side of the house, old fashioned with sideboards and a wooden table and an old gas stove. He fell in love with the place at once, and walked about it, prying into old corners. Whoever had owned it had left no mark. The trustees had removed all traces of personality from the place, and yet it still had a warm, loved air about it. He could imagine wanting to buy it, if he could afford the mortgage.

He had brought some eggs with him and, feeling hungry, he decided to cook himself an omelette for lunch. He found a pan and some plates in a cupboard and knives and forks in a drawer. When he'd cooked the omelette, he went through to the living room and sat on the sofa, gazing out through the French windows at the overgrown paddock beyond.

The paddock there hadn't been touched for years. It was full of long grasses of all different kinds, nettles and thistles, tough bushes and young tree seedlings. He could just see the tall poplar by the side of the house, thrusting up into the sunlight, shimmering with leaves. In fact, the garden was surrounded by trees of all kinds, mostly shorter hedgerow trees, blackthorn and alder, straggly and out-of-hand. At the end of the paddock there were some apple trees, and through a gap beyond, he could see a wheat field with an electric pylon on the far side of it.

He stood up with his plate, deciding to open the French windows and go out on to the little stone area beyond. He looked down for a moment and when he looked up again, he seemed to see a wooden archway he hadn't noticed before. And beyond it he caught a glimpse of the girl, totally absorbed in the ground about her. She was carrying a shoulder-bag. He strained to try to see what she was looking at. And then he realised that the ground all around the place where she was standing was bare, barren earth: nothing would grow in it. She seemed upset by this sterile place. She looked around her in desperation.

Joe put down the plate carefully, determined now to test the reality of what he saw, to prove to himself that this was no hallucination. He would have run straight into the garden, but the French windows were still closed, and proved hard to open. By the time he ran through the bushes to the place where he had seen her, she was gone. There was nothing there at all. The damp ground was overgrown with nettles and tall grass stems. He would have called after her if he had known her name. He looked about again. It was very still, apart from the buzzing of insects in the grass. Then he thought he heard the sound of a car engine. He went quickly to the front of the house, but there was nothing there either. He looked down the road. Was that a glimpse of a red car moving away around the corner? He couldn't be sure. But he felt certain that she had gone.

The first week passed slowly for Joe, and he didn't see the girl again. It was typical English summer weather, warm when the sun shone, but with skies full of fluffy flat-bottomed clouds. There was no telephone, nobody knew where he was, and he felt unexpectedly free of responsibility. At night he lay in the big double bed by the window which overlooked the garden, and his mind lay empty of all thought. He listened to the silence of the place. All he could hear was the rustling of the poplar tree outside his window when the wind blew. It was an aspen and its triangular leaves made a tinkling sound almost like a running stream. One night there was a heavy rain and it pattered and splashed on the tiled roof with a comforting sound. In the morning there was the song of blackbirds and the cooing of wood pigeons in some distant barn.

In the daytime he explored the house and garden. He bought a drawing pad and pencils from the nearby village, and when it was sunny he took a chair on to the stone patch outside the French windows and made sketches of the garden, of the grassy paddock and the waist-high bushes and wild flowers. They were not particularly good drawings but he enjoyed doing them. Occasionally he found himself in need of a human figure in the landscape, and he drew in the figure of the girl. He found a spade and fork in an old lean-to at the side of the house, and began to dig a small square for a garden at one side of the wild paddock where he had seen her. He wondered what he might grow there. He found himself planning for the next year as if the house were already his. He found every little detail of the place strangely moving, as if he was looking at simple things for the very first time. Sometimes he almost imagined he could smell the sea. His thoughts about the house kept quietly interweaving with his thoughts about the girl. The place was full of meaning for him, and time seemed to be slowly emptying out into stillness.

Toward the end of the week he had another dream. He was out at sea, fishing with Tony and Mac. It was peaceful and calm, and they were out in a small boat. Tony held the fishing rods, but it seemed that there was no good bait to attract the fish. Joe had some exceptionally good bait in his pocket, but he wouldn't give it to them. He was pretending that he'd lost it. Mac was getting hostile and was threatening to punch him. Joe was pretending to sulk, and he looked over the boat into the water. The surface was like glass, and he looked down into it. It was unexpectedly beautiful, and absorbing, full of light and colour. He was amazed. There were houses under the water, with lots of little fields full of waving seaweed of different colours, and it was like home. All he had to do to reach it was to drop over the end of the boat and into the water. It would be like entering another world, but it would be home. And he leant further and further over the edge of the boat, and Tony and Mac were shouting at him angrily. So he dropped into the water. It was deep and cool, and he was sinking. And there were great fishes, moving below him, swimming up to meet him. They were of enormous size. And suddenly, because he had the bait, he was frightened.

He woke.

A warm Friday evening found him digging in the garden, preparing the ground for a few strawberry plants perhaps, extending his little square of civilisation into the wild. And as he dug, it occurred to Joe for the first time that people would be starting to worry about him quite a lot. He had not handed in his research; it was locked away, and only he had the key. He checked that it was still in the pocket of his old brown jacket. No one would know where he was. He began to wonder himself why he was refusing to give it up, because that's what it amounted to. He did seem to have some deep instinctual distrust of this research of his, almost a dread. Yet he'd devoted so much time to it, and had succeeded beyond his wildest dreams. At least this technology should open up new choices for the world. The world would be less dependent on fertilisers, on herbicides and pesticides. Surely that must be good. And everyone had told him his discovery could even be the answer to the world's food problems. Why should he doubt it?

Only the future, he supposed, could tell.

He couldn't get out of his mind the image of the girl staring at the barren earth.

*

The whole Superseed idea was a complete disaster, thought Kassy, as she drove down to the cottage on Friday evening. It had been another deeply frustrating week, which reached its climax in another crisis meeting on Friday afternoon. The latest reports from the great wheat and maize fields, and for rice also to a lesser extent, seemed to indicate that a plague of such proportions was developing that it was unlikely there would be any significant cereal harvest at all. It was not just the Third World that could face starvation then. Because the problem had been getting worse over several years, food reserves were running out fast. For some reason Kassy had been driven to remember Joseph, whose intuitions on agricultural management had seen the Pharoahs of Egypt through some lean times. Of course it hadn't stopped the rulers over-exploiting the land in the end; and, with the cedars of Lebanon long gone, the Middle East had mostly become a desert. Most of the planet would be a desert soon, and this time there would be no other land of milk and honey to move on to.

She parked the car round the back of the house and, before doing anything else, she went to look at the garden. But as in all the official seed-trials, there was nothing happening at all. She had brought some more seeds with her, but she didn't feel like planting them now. It would simply be a protest, not an answer. She looked at the soil. Of course there'd been very little rain and the earth was hard and dry, but some of these seeds were supposed to be of a drought-resistant species, some even salt-tolerant. At some point in their history they must have been neglected: moved or stored badly. She felt so betrayed. The whole idea of preserving a heritage, which had so appealed to her when she took on the job, was simply a lie. Her father would say that she was biased by her job, but she knew that the real problem was that broad diversity had not been maintained over the years. The world had become dependent on a few vulnerable monocultures, and that was because of the temptation for profit that the Superseed had provided.

But knowing the problem didn't provide an answer to the future. Only the past, she supposed, could have done that.

She wandered inside and made a cup of tea in the kitchen; and slowly her mind stopped revolving destructively, and she started to unwind as she always did down here, safe from the pressures of the world. She took her tea into the living room and sat on the sofa, and let the peace of the place sink into her.

Through the French windows, the last of the sun had left the dry earth, and was leaving the dusty glass of the empty greenhouse, but was still full on the tall old aspen tree at the side of the house, where the triangular leaves were shimmering and dancing against the blue sky. A moment later she found herself staring idly at the blank telescreen in the room before her and remembering the card in her pocket. She hadn't looked at it all that week, but had kept it to herself. Boff had asked her for it, but she said she had thrown it away, destroyed it. He had been disappointed, but had been forced to accept it. She went over and fed it into the slot. Again she watched her dream unfold in front of her, until the man with the grey eyes was looking at her, and then she stopped it.

She had talked at some length to Boff about dreams. He had said the man was most likely to be some minor figure from her past, whom she had once met or seen, and her mind was using him to represent some greater truth: perhaps a question she should ask herself, or an answer waiting. She rather hoped it was an answer waiting. The rest of the dream was too horrible to leave unanswered. Boff had been very wrapped up all week, seeming to consider himself near to a breakthrough in his thinking on the nature of time and its singularities. He had tried to explain to her, but she had got bogged down in the unfamiliar concepts of Birkhoff's bagels, superstrings and multi-dimensions, and all the bifurcations of strange attractors; all very old-fashioned concepts to Boff, but out of her field. He wanted to experiment more with her dreams, but she had resisted him.

Brilliant as he was, there was something so careless and cavalier about Boff; she didn't always quite trust even her brother with the deeper part of herself. Not that she found trust easy at all, these days.

She left the man's face on the screen, took her tea and wandered upstairs. The warm light of the evening glowed in her bedroom, and gave her comfort. She was tired and would sleep well tonight. She sat on the double bed and looked out of the window again. From here she could see over the hedge at the end of the bare garden, the fields beyond, and the sun on the slowly turning blades of the modern wind-turbines which had replaced the old line of pylons on the national grid. The late sun was still reflecting off the greenhouse roof. And then all of a sudden she saw a man standing in the shadow in the middle of the field, in the midst of the barren soil which she had dug so well. He was leaning on a spade. There was no doubt at all, at that moment, of his absolute reality. She might easily have been frightened. Although the clothes he wore were not the dark green, she might easily have thought it was the Patents Police, come to investigate her. But curiously she wasn't frightened at all. As if he sensed her looking at him, his attention slowly left his spade and the hole he had dug and he looked up towards her, at first above or beyond her somehow, but then suddenly his grey eyes were looking directly into hers. There was a question in his eyes, and something he needed from her.

Quite calmly she left the window and went downstairs to meet him, but when she came out into the garden, he had gone.

She went slowly back into the house, into the living room. On the screen, his face was still looking at her. It was the same man, the same question. She turned off the screen and then took out the card and put it back in her pocket.

Perhaps she had dreamt it all; it was some kind of daydream. It didn't matter. The cottage had always been a place of dreams for her.

*

When Joe first sensed he was being watched, he turned slowly from his digging and looked up at the house. At first he thought it might only have been a squirrel, which moved nervously along the roof-ridge and then ran with a clatter of claws half way down at the tiles, before leaping with easy grace into the poplar tree which shook its leaves in protest. He was reminded painfully of a moment he couldn't place, in his childhood perhaps. Unusual half-connections were crowding into his mind. And it was then he could have sworn he caught a glimpse of the girl at the first-floor window. She was looking straight down at him, it seemed, and then after a moment, withdrew. At once he left his spade, and went into the house, his heart pounding. He leapt up the stairs, two at a time and pushed open the door of the bedroom. But there was no one there. Then he sat on the edge of the double bed for a moment, and looked back down into the garden. He could see the spade he had left, standing upright in the square patch of dark earth. Where had she gone? He started to search the house for her, going into each room in turn, standing still and trying to sense her presence. He knew he was behaving absurdly, but he couldn't stop himself.

At last he went back to the garden and looked up again at the house. There was nothing there now, but his heart was still beating strongly. He was full of the most certain knowledge that she was somehow the key to his understanding. He would not be in this place at all, had she not led him there. He stood still in the overgrown garden for a long time. Slowly the sun left the top of the tall aspen tree and it began to get dark.

Then he put the spade away behind the green door of the lean-to and went back into the house and slowly up the stairs. Now he could feel her presence all around the house. It was quite irrational, this closeness he felt. His mind told him he must be going insane. It was time to go to bed. After a good night's sleep, this sudden strange obsession might have passed.

*

Kassy undressed slowly, almost in a dream. It was such a warm evening so she opened the windows as wide as she could and then sat in the window in her nightdress. Leaning back, she watched the last of the sun leave the top of the old aspen tree, while she tried to puzzle out what this trick of her mind could mean.

He had been digging with the spade in her garden. In some way she felt encouraged by it, felt that he was on her side, close to her, trying like her to grow something there, despite all failures. And she felt less alone than she had for years. She waited, half expecting to see him again in the garden, but not minding if she didn't, while the sky darkened. She listened for the sound of the sea. Sometimes you could hear it, even above the noise of the wind turbines across the field, or the rustling of the aspen leaves, if the wind was in the right direction. But now it was very still; the windmills were hardly moving at all, and the sea was probably like glass. She could smell the sea in the night air though.

She went to the bathroom, and ran a bath; the water was really hot now after such a sunny day and she soaked in it for a long time. When she came back the bedroom was quite dark; she knelt on the bed and looked out of the window again. The night was exceptionally warm and becoming quite, quite still. It was almost as if time itself were slowing to a standstill, or emptying its meaning into the space around her till the night was full to bursting.

She thought of Boff's theories about singularities of time, how communication might be possible across the deeps of time – like whales sending out long, slow sound pictures across the oceans – how thoughts and feelings might merge, and so at last bring even physical bodies together. Boff believed that such singularities were mathematically possible, in certain conditions, especially if the space, and the emotional mood coincided. But what would it do to the rest of the world?

The night seemed to be getting hotter, and even stiller. There was a sound like flowing water in her ears. She slipped off her nightdress and slid down between the clean, fresh sheets. As she settled herself to sleep a great sureness came over her, a feeling that the world was good, that she was somehow in control of her life, a feeling she had not felt for a very long time. And she remembered Boff telling her how whales make love, picking each other out as individual soul mates over vast distances, locking in on each other's songs, how joyful their sensuous foreplay when they met, and how they finally mated face to face like humans, as they rose out of the water, by the sublime power of their enormous tail-flukes.

Somewhere, beyond time, she fancied, two whales had heard each other's songs and were turning, beginning their race to find each other, across the wide ocean.

And from the pillow she watched the indigo blue sky darken into night and the light of the stars strengthen in the darkness.

Then faintly, out of the stillness, she thought she heard the soft splash of water. She waited but she didn't hear it again. Turning in her bed, she looked towards the open bedroom door. Across the tiny landing, there was a light on, under the bathroom door. She must have left the light on.

And now there seemed to be the faint slap and splash of water moving gently in the bath. She lay for a moment, calmly trying to think if she could be dreaming or imagining things.

Then the noise seemed to stop, and she felt reassured. Nevertheless, the fact that she had left the light on preyed on her mind. After a little while, she could bear it no longer and got out of bed.

But before she could reach her bedroom door, the bathroom door opened. For some reason, she was quite unafraid, as if she half expected it. For a moment before he turned out the bathroom light, she saw him coming out through the steam, his slender body as vulnerable as a boy's. Their eyes met. For a split second they both stood there naked, before the light went off and they were together in the darkness.

But then he had gone. She stood for a long time by the door of the bedroom, feeling confused. Then she moved forward and turned on the bathroom light for a moment. The bathroom was empty, cool and dry. She waited some time, her heart beating violently. There was nothing there. It had all been in her mind. Slowly she turned and went back to bed.

The bed was warm in the heat of the night. She felt the strangest yearning, and a need for comfort before she slept.

*

He seemed to feel the gift of her presence all night. The unusual warmth of his bed made him restless; the whole room seemed to grow warmer, so that he had to get up in the night to open the window. The first isolated blackbird out in the fields was just beginning to call at the first hint of a lightening of the darkness. But the open window made him no less restless, and the room was no less warm, till there was a moment in the pale dawn when he woke suddenly out of a half sleep; he opened his eyes and found himself looking straight into her eyes, her fair hair on the pillow beside him, her body alongside his. But as he reached out to touch her, he knew it was unreal, and he was alone again; so that he turned away and pressed his body into the bed, overflowing with the deepest frustration.

*

As the lights of dawn slowly grew, Kassy slept and dreamt. She was alone on a desert island where she had been for many years. The sand was white and hot. Then she started to walk into the sea, and she knew this was a brave thing to do, because once she was in the sea she would be utterly changed and never be able to go back to her island again. But the water was cool and inviting and rose up her thighs and washed between her legs and then she suddenly lost her footing and dropped; her head was under water and she had stepped off a coral precipice into the deep, where great fishes swam. Great dim forms far below turned slowly up towards her. And she was frightened then that she might drown and she woke. It was full dawn now, and she was alone, naked on the bed, the sheets in a tangle on the floor. It was still very warm. She searched for her clock on the bedside table and it was half past six.

She got up and threw a dressing gown around her, and sleepily went down to the kitchen to make herself something to drink. And as she found her way down the stairs, she heard a knock at the front door of the cottage.

*

Joe's bed was a crumpled mess of sheets and blankets. He looked at his watch and it was half past six.

He got up and threw a dressing gown round him and sleepily went down to the kitchen to make himself some tea. As he moved down the stairs in that strange half-state between sleeping and waking, he too heard a knock at the front door.

He had the strangest sensation that it had something to do with her.

Kassy knew at once it had something to do with him. For a moment they were together, at the bottom of the stairs, converging, moving towards the front door together, in almost perfect synchronicity their hands stretching out to take the handle, to turn the lock, thinking of each other, no other thoughts in their heads, their minds and bodies almost together…

Something is shifting slightly in the deep fabric of time, like the very first stirrings of an earthquake, far below.

Under the deepest ocean, there are mountain ranges vaster than the Himalayas. But the tops of their highest peaks are almost deeper than thought can reach down, and they lie under a pressure too crushing for life, in a darkness too thick for sight. Along these ocean ridges lie undersea volcanoes. Sometimes, from the unconscious core of the earth, the magma rises, bursting its way through miles of solid rock until it erupts into the ocean, fire and water meeting in explosions of unimaginable size, forcing apart the continental plates and changing the carefully learnt geography of the ocean floor. Violent seismic shocks move through thousands of miles of sea like lightning, offending the subtle tuning for gentler sound; huge, mysterious patches of heat bubble up to disturb the shape of the sea, so that all bearings may be lost. There is a fearful power to be released at the meeting of two worlds.

Everything we have ever taken for granted may hang in the balance.

But then the cottage door was opened. Kassy was looking into the hard eyes of a green-uniformed policeman. The man said: 'Get your things and come with me, miss. Now.'

Joe was looking at Tony, standing defiantly on the doorstep. His friend said: 'Joe! Where the hell have you been?'

And their worlds were split apart.

CHAPTER FIVE

'HOW DID YOU FIND ME?' said Joe.

'You may well ask.' Tony was not pleased.

'Come in then,' said Joe sheepishly, and shuffled into the kitchen to make a cup of tea.

'What the hell are you playing at Joe? The whole firm's gone mad, running about like headless chickens.'

'I was told to take a holiday,' said Joe deviously, as he busied himself with tea making.

Tony watched him incredulously. 'You've no idea of the panic that's set in at HQ. Mac thinks you've been kidnapped by a rival biotech business.'

'How did you find me?' said Joe again, trying to deflect him.

'That was a saga in itself. You must be the most secretive bugger in the Western world. You should work for MI5. What is this? A safe house? And where the hell do you leave the key to your flat? You must have some friends or neighbours you leave it with, for emergencies. No? We got so desperate by the end of the week, we forced our way in. Up a ladder. Through a window. Police there and everything. By a pure miracle you left the details of this place lying about on the sofa, so I thought I'd try it.'

'You've been burgling my flat!' said Joe, almost laughing at the absurdity of it, but beginning to realise, with a sinking heart, that his so-called holiday was over.

'Well everybody wants to know where your research is for one thing –'

'Why didn't you ask Carol?'

'I did. She couldn't find it in your desk.'

It was Joe's turn to feel angry. 'Bloody hell, why haven't you broken into all my other files? Why don't you ask the police for a search warrant?'

'Oh, come on Joe, we're just worried about you. Concerned.'

There was a pause. Joe poured out the tea, and Tony sat at the kitchen table.

'Well, I admit to some selfish interest,' went on Tony, and now he grinned. 'I'm off in a few days. I want to take some of this stuff with me. Do my credit no end of good with governments and big landowners. I've a lot of African and Asian capitals to cover in the next few months. I must get off to a good start....'

As Tony rattled on in the usual 'company' way, Joe's mind wandered. He realised how far away from it all he now felt. Something seemed to be dropping into place because of this last week at the cottage. Doubts that had crossed his mind before, but that he'd never dwelt on. For all its technical advantages, this 'Superseed' idea could be used as just another subtler way of cornering the market; and if so, it might only lead to more centralisation, uniformity and dependence. Perhaps they should be devoting their energies to custom-built improvements to local plants, increasing diversity and independence, not destroying it. For some reason he thought suddenly and vividly of the girl. He seemed to see her in handcuffs, driven away by the police. A symbol of the shackled future.

'Just a minute!' he said sharply.

Tony stopped in mid-sentence. 'What is it?' he asked.

'Can you hear anything?' Unmistakeably now, Joe could hear the sound of a car, pulling out of the drive.

'Nothing,' said Tony. 'It's dead quiet here, isn't it?'

Joe strained to look out of the window and then ran to the front door. But he could see nothing. Tony's flash car was next to his little Renault in the drive, but that was all. He returned slowly to the kitchen.

'Did you hear a car?' he said.

Tony looked really concerned. 'Joe,' he said, 'are you all right?'

There was a long silence.

'I don't know,' he answered eventually.

'I wish you'd talk to me. It's no good bottling everything up.'

And with a shock Joe realised that here was the man who was supposed to be his best friend in all the world, and there was no possibility that he could unburden himself about anything that mattered to him now. His desperate need for space; his doubts about his own research, or rather the uses to which it might be put; his half-formed despair about the future; above all, his visions of this girl and how she seemed to tie in with all of this – to his friend this would all appear as madness. Even to him it seemed absurd. Perhaps he did need a psychiatrist, but the fact was that some strange intuition told him that if he could share this girl's understanding, everything would clarify in his mind and his way forward would become clear. He wanted to unburden himself to her, and yet she was just a vision in his head, unreal. So why did she feel more real and close and important to him than Tony, his best friend, sitting here in front of him? Perhaps he really was going insane.

Tony watched his friend, as he stood there pale and staring. Joe had always been a somewhat obsessive character, but this was becoming frightening. He got up and put his arms round him.

'Joe, you old idiot. You've been working far too hard. Let go, for God's sake.'

'I'm sorry,' said Joe. He felt at a loss.

'Come on,' said Tony encouragingly.

'I've nothing much to say that would make sense.'

'Did you see the doctor?'

'Yes.'

'What did he say?'

'Take a holiday. I'm trying.' He smiled and repeated himself with emphasis: 'I *am trying.*'

'Well you'll have to come back to town sometime today, if only to give in your research. But then you can come back for as long as you like. Or why not come with me to Cairo? Hey, there's an idea! You could have a break, see the pyramids, while I work! Then there's the nightlife… It's not good for you to be on your own all the time. By the way, have you been in touch with Sarah?'

'No.'

'Poor girl, she'll pine away. She needs it and she needs it from you.' Joe laughed despite himself and Tony pressed on. 'Come on. Come back to the real world. Here, show me round this place. How are you managing?'

Joe showed him round the cottage. Tony declared it to be a bit primitive. He asked Joe where he did his shopping and Joe told him about the local village. They wandered out into the overgrown garden and down to the gap in the hedge where they looked across the neighbouring field to the line of pylons. Joe declared his interest in buying the cottage, if he could get a mortgage on it. He was sick of renting, he said. He could easily commute into Cambridge... Soon Joe had returned to the world of easy banter, and Tony began to be reassured.

'But you must come up to town tonight. Everybody's getting dead worried. Hand in the research and reassure everybody that you're not going off your head. I must be going soon, and I want your promise before I go.'

'Well, I....'

'Sacred promise.'

This implied an ancient hand ritual from their under-graduate days; usually invoked for deep secrets, or outrageous dares. Joe laughed.

'All right,' he said. 'I promise to come back to Cambridge tonight!' And the ritual was performed.

'Good.' said Tony. 'We can't have you going off your head, or you might lose your job. And then where will you be?'

But though Tony spoke lightly, Joe sensed a lurking threat behind the words. He was being put under pressure by his pay-masters. And his resistance to it was growing by the minute.

*

Kassy felt a moment of great panic when she saw the patents officer at the door. She felt the fear that occupied people feel when the dawn police raid strikes. But curiously, the officer didn't search the house, or investigate the back garden, where she felt there were buried enough infringements of the law to cause her to lose her job, and put her in prison for years. He simply waited patiently for her in the narrow hallway, while she collected her things together; and she began to realise that this was a subtler game.

From the bathroom upstairs, she could see a dark green van outside with several other policemen still in it. It seemed she was not being arrested for the attempt to grow illegal plants, at least not yet. She didn't argue, or hesitate, but obeyed everything without question, as she had been taught to do. Even though she was the daughter of a powerful father, she could never have argued with the Patents Police.

She was allowed to drive her own red car back to town, but the officer insisted on sitting beside her. And she was forced to follow the dark green van all the way back to Cambridge. As they drove back she glanced occasionally at the deadpan face of the officer beside her, till she could bear it no longer.

'What is it then?' she asked. 'Am I being arrested?'

The man beside her smiled briefly, in a mournful sort of way. 'It's all right, miss,' he said. 'It's orders from up high. Nothing to worry about.'

'Where are you taking me?'

'Superseed House.'

'On a Saturday?'

'Don't ask me, miss, I'm only carrying out orders.'

The countryside seemed quiet and deserted, even for a Saturday. The toll-road checkpoint was automatic but there was usually somebody about. Today the world might have been asleep. The sun was rising through the haze and the little car was getting warm as they passed the Superseed hoarding.

GIVE US THIS DAY OUR DAILY BREAD

She checked that the officer beside her still wore his hat, put on her own, and opened up the roof. She kept her eye on the back of the van in front, on the black 'PP' across the doors and the small barred windows, while the monotonous miles of wheat passed by, unrelieved by any features. The fields seemed more still and empty than ever.

Then suddenly over on her right, she noticed a plume of smoke rising, and at the same moment she heard a sharp, hoarse scream rise up over the plain like the cry of a marsh bird in pain. She felt unnerved by it, and the car swerved slightly.

'What was that?' she asked.

'I didn't hear anything,' said the man. But surely he must have heard it.

She tried to look to her right, but she could only see the smoke rising. It was not unlike the way they sometimes used to burn the stubble after the harvest, except that such practices were illegal now. Then came the unmistakable crackle of laser fire.

'What is it?' she asked more insistently.

'Routine exercises,' said the man, and for some reason her blood ran cold. 'All in defence of freedom. I think it might be better if you closed the sunroof, miss.'

'Why?' she asked, finding herself irritated by the man.

'Just do it please, miss.'

She obeyed. The road was empty ahead except for the green van, and now a gap seemed to be opening between them. The green van was speeding away.

'Keep up,' said the man beside her, harshly, and then she knew that he too was nervous.

She drove faster, to try to close the gap. The fiftieth anniversary balloon was hanging over the North Checkpoint, looking ever larger as they approached, and from this side she could clearly read its advertisement, gold lettering on red.

NOTHING SUCCEEDS LIKE SUPERSEEDS

That old motto, the oldest of all, seemed very inappropriate at the moment.

As they came up to the checkpoint, she thought she caught a glimpse of a body lying in the ditch at the side of the road. It might have been a tramp asleep, but crumpled up in a strange way. She decided to say nothing to the deadpan face beside her. They didn't even have to stop at the checkpoint. Kassy was surprised. The barrier rose and closed again at once behind them. They were not even asked for their passes, but were waved quickly through, almost as if they were expected. There were more green uniforms there than ever; but they sped on, along the deserted early-morning streets towards Parkside, and Superseed House.

When they drew up, the man beside her simply said, 'Goodbye, miss,' and got out, walking forward to join his colleagues in the van in front, while the driver's door was opened for her by a man in a grey suit whom she recognised as one of her father's security staff. She knew now where she was going. She left the red car parked outside and followed him into the familiar foyer. They took the lift straight up to the penthouse.

Weekend or not, her father was deep at work – gazing into his computer on top of his huge desk in the alcove at the far side of the room.

'Come in. Come in. I'm sorry to do this to you, but it seemed the only appropriate response.'

'To what?'

'A spot of local trouble. Only I know you don't always take things seriously enough, so I thought it better to make sure.'

He was still absorbed by his PC.

She felt the anger rising in her already.

'What do you mean?'

'I'm sorry, littl'un; you can be angry with me if you like, but you don't know the situation…' At last he turned. 'Since you left last night, there has been very ugly rioting all over. But Cambridge has been a special target – because of this place, of course. I suppose the idiots think we have all kinds of answers here which might grow into instant miracles in their back gardens. Probably our own fault in a way: they've come to depend on us too much, and now that we don't have any easy answers, they're disappointed. The basis of riots and revolutions since history began, of course. 'Give us bread,' all that sort of thing. No thought for what it costs to make bread. Everybody wants something for nothing. It comes from watching too much television. They will show all these pictures of starving babies. It doesn't help anybody to a rational solution. The sooner they bring in these new broadcasting laws, the better for everybody. Showing riots is one thing, it can help to make viewers annoyed with those who stir up trouble; but what defence have you got against a starving baby? It only goes to spread despair…'

Her father never talked so much usually, Kassy thought; he must be rattled.

'Anyway, last night there was a hell of a riot in the city. God knows how the demonstrators got in. Smashed a few windows at the back, nothing serious. But I don't think it's safe for any staff to be outside now, especially when we don't really know what's going on out there.'

Kassy was silent. She sat in one of the cream armchairs.

Eventually she said: 'I see. Thank you, Dad.'

'That's all right, littl'un.' She wished he wouldn't call her that. He only did it in private, called her by his pet name of childhood, but she hated it now.

'The fact is,' he went on, 'we're all used to thinking of Cambridge as a sacrosanct scientific area, but it may not be that for much longer. And a lot of people know that red car, and who drives it. It could become a target for terrorists.'

'I see. Well, thank you for warning me, Dad.'

'That's all right, littl'un. Let's have some coffee.'

He went over to his desk and pressed a button on his computer.

'Let's just hope the PP can keep everything quiet, till we can sort out an answer.'

They fell silent. Jonas was clearly nervous and kept looking to the door.

'Where the devil's Ranji got to?' he said at last.

Ranji, the Indian servant, seemed to be missing, so Kassy went out to the kitchen to make the coffee herself.

When she came back with it, her father was already involved again at the computer screen. Kassy put a cup on the desk and sat back on the sofa. She wondered if any terrorist would be interested in her base collection, and part of her wished it were worth a terrorist's interest. Idly, she glanced at the old portraits of eminent people on the wall behind her father's desk, the founding fathers of Superseed. And she thought, where could the answer lie to all this horror?

Suddenly a cold sensation down her spine held her rigid with shock. She was looking straight into the face of the man with the grey eyes. He looked older, his hair was shorter, nearly white, there were more wrinkles around his eyes, but it was unmistakably him. He was looking at her out of a framed portrait on the wall to the right of her father's desk. She stared in disbelief.

'Dad,' she said at last.

It took a moment for her to capture his attention. She pointed at the painting. 'Who's that?'

'Good Lord,' he said. 'I am ashamed by your lack of knowledge sometimes. Don't you know?'

'No.'

'That's Joe Goodman.'

'Has that picture always been there?'

'Yes, since you were a child. You must have noticed it before.'

Probably, she thought. So Boff was right. Her mind had picked a face she hardly knew and put it into her dreams. But what was the significance to her of Joe Goodman, inventor of the original Superseed? Her mind was racing. Her father now seemed to welcome the interruption. He had got up and stood in front of his desk.

'Yes, I've always kept these paintings over my desk as an inspiration. Helps me not to forget the essentials. Mac McAndrew in the middle: the first Chief Executive, a brilliant man. Tony Woolf on the left, first Sales Director – a warrior in the field; Joe Goodman, first Chief Scientist. He was the greatest of them in my view.'

Kassy kept silent while her father started to expand on his knowledge of history, talking as if he were making notes for an essay.

'He was one of the great geneticists of all time. Won the Nobel prize for the invention of the Superseed range. Spent his life on the few basic cereal crops, wheat, rice, maize, sorghum and so on, and developed a Superstrain for all of them. Started out here I believe. Later he went to America. Had a huge army of scientists working for him by the end. Died, sadly, before the sudden great climate changes in the '20s. Could have helped the world a lot then.'

Could have helped the corporation, thought Kassy. She noticed her father often said the world when he meant the corporation. As Jonas talked, Kassy felt increasingly confused. This man, Joe Goodman, was one of the founding fathers of Superseed. He must have believed passionately in what he was doing, creating a superior monoculture to conquer the world for profit. And now when she was coming to question the whole transnational idea of monoculture, how could this man possibly hold out any answers for her? She felt strangely betrayed, irrational as it was. She hated this man for having sold his soul to Superseed all those years ago. He was as bad as her father and with less excuse. An enemy. She felt angry and confused, and wanted to send him to hell.

'If only he was around now,' her father was saying, 'he might have some answers for us.'

'I don't see why,' she said quickly.

'He was a great scientist. There's a whole chapter on him in the first volume – 'The Technical Breakthrough' – don't you remember it?'

Kassy shrugged.

'You should,' said her father.

Kassy didn't like to admit that she rarely did more than skim through her father's beloved books. The sustained reading of history bored her, perhaps because it fascinated her father. In any case, she was certain that anything written about Joe Goodman by an official Superseed historian would be pure hagiography.

'We certainly need a man like him now,' her father said, and went back to his PC.

Kassy sat there for a little, still feeling stunned. Then she found herself remembering the look on Joe's face in her dream; and then as she had seen it when he was digging the garden. The question he seemed to be asking her. She suddenly couldn't believe that this man would want all this mass starvation as a vision of his future. She felt she must somehow interpret the message he had for her. The answer must lie back in the cottage. She stood up.

'Dad,' she began, 'I've left a few things down at the cottage.'

'What things?' he said absently.

She hesitated. If she said personal things, he wouldn't take it seriously enough. 'Just a few papers,' she said at last, 'but they're quite important to me. If I go straight away now, I promise I'll be back in an hour or so. Before lunch, I should think.'

'I'm sorry, littl'un, but it's out of the question. I've given orders that you're not to leave town.'

'You've what?'

'Given orders that you should stay here. It's far too dangerous to go back. Really.'

'You could give me an escort.'

'Can't spare the personnel.' After a moment he said, 'It's for your own good.' There was a hardness in his voice now.

Suddenly she felt desperate to escape.

'I don't understand. You've virtually arrested me, brought me back here under armed guard, and now you won't let me go back. Don't you trust me?'

'Ah, now there's a question…'

He turned to face her.

She found herself going very cold.

'What is it Dad?'

He spoke gently. 'You're an employee of this corporation, littl'un, but more than that, you're my daughter. I don't expect difficulties from you of all people.'

'What do you mean?'

'If I can't rely on your loyalty, where am I? You're in a very high-profile job. I didn't give it to you lightly. You're holding in your gene banks the heritage of the Third World. That's very important.'

'I know that, Dad, that's why I –'

'Well, lately I've sometimes felt that your heart's not really in it.'

'What do you mean?'

'I put my own daughter there for a very specific purpose. To reassure the Third World that their heritage is in good hands. To reassure them on the question of diversity.'

'Reassure them?' Kassy couldn't believe what she was hearing. 'I would love to be able to reassure them,' she said. 'But what reassurance could I possibly give them on the question of diversity? None of the wild seeds which were so carefully collected over half a century ago show any sign of germination at all.'

'That's not the point, littl'un. Never has been.'

'What is the point?'

'We're in a dangerous political situation now, and we've got to stick together. There are idiots out there who want to grow anything but Superseeds. On principle. You could give them hope and comfort holding the views you do. You've got to support the corporation. All I ask is that you keep a low profile and say we're trying to maintain diversity and hold your fire until the scientists come up with an answer.'

'Are you trying to tell me I've only ever been a front to pacify the Third World?'

'Of course not, I'm not saying –'

'Are you going to sack me then, if I disobey you?'

'Don't be silly, that would send quite the wrong signals. But you must see the sense of what I'm saying. Listen, because I'm your father –'

'Does that mean I'm supposed to have no ideas of my own?'

He tried to calm her. 'Now, littl'un…'

'Don't you dare call me littl'un! Don't you dare…' She was suddenly speechless with rage. 'I'm not your…'

'Now calm down,' her father went on, softly and evenly, trying to put his hands on her shoulders. 'These are difficult times for all of us, and we must try –'

'How could you? These aren't difficult times for you. They may be difficult times for the starving, perhaps, but not for you or me –'

He was now holding her by the shoulders. 'Getting emotional won't help –'

'Damn you, let me go –'

'Please, littl'un –'

There was a kind of screaming inside her as she shook free of him, and backed away. 'I hate you sometimes, Dad, I really hate you.'

He replied calmly still, but his voice shook, and he had a curious lopsided smile.

'I might have known you'd let me down in a crisis,' he said. 'Sometimes I wish you'd never been born. All I ever wanted was a loyal son to follow in my footsteps.'

Kassy froze. It was some time before he spoke again. Spoke to hurt her, but also out of the depth of his own disappointment.

'I wanted you to be a boy, you know, but it was your mother's first child and she wanted a girl. It was a new technology then, so I gave way. I thought there'd be plenty of time for more children. But if I'd known I'd never really have the son I wanted…'

Kassy stood and looked at him, aware that every word spoken split open a wound between them that couldn't be healed. A child needs to be loved absolutely, but there's no such thing as absolute love, except in our dreams.

'I hate you!' she screamed, and turned and ran from the office. But as she ran, her father shook his head and walked back slowly to reach for the telephone on his desk.

As if by some political reflex, he was still slightly smiling.

But Kassy was too quick for him. In her urgent need to escape, she hurled herself into the open lift and took it rapidly to the ground floor. As she ran across the foyer, she noticed the receptionist leaning across to answer a ringing telephone. But then she was through the swing doors and out into the street. There, the little red car was waiting still, where she had left it. A security guard was standing next to it, but did not question her use of it. As she pulled away from the kerb, several men in green uniforms burst out of the building on to the street. She drove off as fast as she could with no firm idea in her head, beyond getting away out of the city and back to the cottage, even though she knew in her heart that her freedom could not last long.

She drove rapidly along the familiar route, noticing nothing unusual or different, except perhaps the greater number of uniforms on the street. It might have been an ordinary quiet Saturday morning. Her first indication that something was wrong was as she drew nearer to the North Checkpoint. The big Superseed advertising balloon there was in flames. The gold lettering was obliterated in a whirling mass of black smoke and flickering red fire. Pieces of flaming rubber were dropping down on to the checkpoint below. This sight should perhaps have warned her to turn back, but the only precaution she took was to close fast the windows of her car. As she came round a corner a moment later and accelerated towards the checkpoint, she found herself driving the red car towards a solid mass of shouting demonstrators who spanned the road from side to side. They were marching towards her in defiant solidarity. Subliminally she took in some of the placards: 'No to Superseed', 'Bread for Everyone'; but mostly she only saw their chanting faces, swollen with fury and hatred as they marched on the city.

She put her foot over the brake, hesitating. She had been instantly aware of both the power and the vulnerability of the rich girl's car, as this crowd would see it. Had she time to stop and turn around before they came to envelop her? She felt she would surely have to crawl back to her father then. Or should she accelerate into the crowd, forcing them to make way for her? Beyond them, she could glimpse the checkpoint itself, only a hundred yards or so down the road, the barriers broken, the perimeter wires chopped, guardhouse and outbuildings smashed and flaming, the way open.

For a moment the crowd seemed to part a little more. In the space beyond, green-uniformed men lay strewn about the road among the debris of their shattered outpost. More rioters were streaming in through the broken barriers, but there seemed for a moment a good chance of escape. She put her foot down on the accelerator and the car leapt forward. Surprised faces reared up at her, but a way seemed miraculously to open up in front of her.

She tried to hold her nerve steady, but suddenly there was a sickening bump on the nearside wing of the car and the clatter of a falling placard on the roof. Ahead of her, the crowd seemed almost to be thickening; it was all around her now. The placard bounced along the roof of the car, and fell down, obscuring for a moment the back windscreen. Another thump on the other side of the car as someone else was struck. But now the crowd was opening up and she accelerated again. Jesus Christ, she thought grimly, what am I doing? Straight ahead on the ground she could see the prostrate body of a green-uniformed policeman. She couldn't tell if he was dead or not. Swerving to avoid him, she felt the car bumping over his ankles. A fair-headed boy in glasses ahead seemed unable to know which way to jump and started screaming. Kassy's nerve broke and she swerved again and slammed her foot on the brakes. The car slewed sideways, missing the boy by inches, and she almost lost control of it, but it straightened up at last, while the boy's fallen glasses slid about on the bonnet of the car, miraculously unbroken. Then the car reared up over some debris and skidded almost to a standstill, perhaps twenty yards from the burning checkpoint. She tried to move forward again, but the crowd were rapidly moving in on her now, growing denser all around her, and a moment later she was forced to a dead stop.

The windows were closed already, but she quickly locked the doors and then sat paralysed with terror, her heart racing, wondering what she should do next. How could she reason with these people now, tell them she was on their side? The faces gathered round the car, peering in at every window. It seemed someone might have recognised the red car as her father's, and they were already speculating as to who she might be. A fat man was sprawling over the bonnet now, making obscene movements and leering at her. His big hands took the boy's glasses which had become entangled in the windscreen wipers and crushed them in front of her face. Someone else started rhythmically banging on the boot of the car with the flat of his hand. There was aggressive laughter.

All at once the crowd grew quieter, and heads turned. Someone seemed to be pushing their way to the front of the crowd, seemed to be taking charge. A man appeared beside the car; and Kassy recognised, with a shock, her father's servant Ranji.

'Come out of there,' he ordered to her above the noise of the crowd.

Her mind wouldn't work clearly. Was it safer to disobey and remain inside the car, or should she risk facing the mob? Ranji made up her mind for her with a quick movement. He lifted some heavy metal object in his hand, and the window next to the driving seat shattered all over her. At once several rough hands were pushing in, searching for the lock. A moment later and she was dragged out of the car and pulled to one side.

She tried to keep on her feet. The fat man and two of his friends were rocking the red car from side to side, working up the momentum to turn it over. Kassy herself was being pushed and nudged and shouted at from all sides while Ranji looked on. People were asking her where she lived, what was her name, but she found she couldn't answer.

Then she was grabbed painfully by the shoulders and forced down on her knees. The fat man put his face up to hers and there was the foul smell of his breath. She thought she would probably be killed now and she knew she was powerless. Time appeared to go into slow motion, and she seemed to watch herself almost from outside her body, as she waited to be raped or torn to pieces by the jostling, sweaty bodies around her.

*

Joe, meanwhile, was driving reluctantly on his way back to town. He had managed to shake Tony off with promises; but then, after Tony had gone, he had quickly decided that there was no way he could avoid going back to face up to everything. So he'd packed up a few things and had started out soon after him. He hoped to make it a quick visit and then be back at the cottage as soon as possible. He would put everyone at their ease, leave his address, see Mac, perhaps give him the research to look after… Perhaps. But there was a hollow feeling in his heart.

And suddenly the strongest intuition of danger.

He slowed the car. There was nothing wrong. The long straight road stretched away ahead of him, the chequered fields and woods on either side. There was a certain amount of traffic coming out of town on the other carriageway, but the road was not especially busy. It was a typical grey summer's day. There seemed nothing wrong or unusual anywhere. Then he noticed up ahead of him, in the distance, a strange shape hanging over the road. He couldn't make it out. A moment later, it seemed to have gone. He thought perhaps it might have been a light aeroplane, spraying the crops with insecticide. He remembered the film of *North by Northwest*. He drove on still more slowly, suffocated by this strange intuitive fear. He couldn't place it, but wondered if it had something to do with the girl.

Then, in a flash, he saw it again, now much closer, hanging over the road. It was a huge red balloon, like one of the balloons in his dream. And there was writing on it which he couldn't yet make out. He felt a strange weakness, flooding his body. The balloon was so real. To see images from real life in your dreams is common, he thought, but to see images from your dreams in real life... Yet that's what seemed to be happening to him more and more often; in the lab, at the cottage...

Then he could make out the words on the balloon. They read:

NOTHING SUCCEEDS LIKE SUPERSEEDS

It was the joke that Tony had made. And at the very moment he read those words the balloon burst into flames. The dream symbolism was so obvious that he made the connection at once. He found himself slowing the car almost to a standstill. The balloon was still there, hanging over the road. Black smoke was pouring out of it and flickering red flames. Huge pieces of flaming rubber were dripping from it. The sight was so unnerving that he forced himself to look down, and concentrate on the road ahead. When he looked back it was gone, as if it had never been. A daylight dream.

He drove on shakily towards the city and all the time the feeling of dread grew on him. He left the dual carriageway and soon after became aware that the road ahead seemed to be blocked. He tried to make out the obstacle. Perhaps there had been an accident. He supposed so; there seemed to be debris scattered everywhere. He was going to be the first car on the scene. He felt panic; perhaps all he had been feeling was the premonition of a real disaster. As he approached he drew over to the side of the road. He stopped and got out of the car.

When he looked again the scene seemed to have grown in complexity. A red car must have crashed. It was turned over on its side in the middle of the road. There were one or two people lying on the ground. One man wore green overalls and his ankles were smashed. There was blood everywhere. Half dazed, Joe began to walk down the road towards the scene.

Then suddenly his mind took in the whole scene at once. He recognised the red car: it belonged to the girl, he was sure of it. And then there she was on her knees, surrounded by people trying, it seemed, to help her to her feet. But it was no ordinary accident. There were banners everywhere. It was a demonstration. Yet it was absolutely silent, an eerie world, like a film without a soundtrack. He could read what the banners said though. 'No to Superseed' and 'Smash the Superseed'. And he could see hands reaching down to the girl.

And then the sound came into his mind. The screaming of hoarse voices, the wailing of a police siren in the distance. All of a sudden the red car burst into flames with a roar and the crowd scattered away from it. A large man stripped to the waist lay crying out on the ground, too close to the burning car to escape from it. His chest and one shoulder had been badly crushed by something. Flailing about like a beached whale, he was smearing his blood on the road around him. Somewhere further away Joe could hear the chant of the demonstrators.

'Superseed, Seed of Strife,

Give us back the Seeds of Life!'

And now he could hear, above all the noise, the girl was crying out to the people around her. 'I'm on your side!' she was screaming. 'My name's Kassy. I can help you. Please. I agree with you. I don't believe in Superseed.' And it was then that he knew that the crowd around her were not trying to help her, but to kill her. They were pushing her and picking at her skirt. One Asian man alone seemed to be keeping the rest of them at bay.

Joe broke into a run, but as in the way of dreams, he hardly seemed to be making progress at all. Time seemed to be slowing down. He called out to her – 'Kassy!' – and she seemed to hesitate and turned and looked straight towards him; confused.

'Help me!' she said. And then called out his name. 'Joe?'

Even as he ran he thought, she knows my name. And she was trying to hold out a hand to him. Now her attackers were turning and looking towards him too, as he tried to fling himself into the crowd around her; and through the crowd, he stretched out to take her hand.

But before they could reach each other, time seemed to empty out of the moment, and everything slowed to a standstill.

Unmistakably now, something cracks in the bedrock of Time, and huge forces shift, if only the better to hold back some unimaginable power.

In spite of distance, in spite of darkness, two minds have heard each other's song and have already turned; have begun their race to find each other across the wide ocean. They have sent out signals through the deep – ultrasonic booms of such power and precision that only they can foresee the result. And just as they can sense the seismic shocks from the hidden mountain ridges of the ocean floor echoing back across the deep, so now they can feel the violent inner shocks from the potential reshaping of time; the melted magma of possible new time bubbling up from the depths, white hot, to shift all past and future certainties. But they know this is only the slightest hint of a greater explosion to come and they simply adjust their bearings, hardly swerving a fraction of a degree on their determined course.

And still their minds go on seeking each other out, moving steadily towards each other, whatever the darkness, whatever the distance.

Joe stood alone in the middle of the road, screaming.

'No to Superseed!' he found himself shouting. His arms were outstretched into thin air, and it seemed that he had stopped the traffic in both directions.

'No to Superseed!'

People were getting out of their cars and gathering round to stare curiously at this madman performing his antics. Some of them were smiling in mild amusement. This kind of diatribe was not entirely unknown from religious maniacs, or drunken outcasts, though not usually in the middle of a busy main road. Nevertheless, they kept their distance.

Joe stopped then, and stood abashed and looked about him. There was something of a tailback now on both sides of the road. There were perhaps ten or twenty sober-looking people gathered around him in a wide irregular circle, staring at him blankly, objectively, waiting for his next move. He took in a fat man with a coarse, aggressive face, and a fair-haired boy with glasses. A workman was wearing green overalls.

A moment later a black car moved up smoothly into the circle. There was the bang of a car door. Joe felt a hand on his arm, and heard Tony's voice.

'Come on, me old mate.'

Joe stood very still, and tried to collect his thoughts.

'My car's back there,' he said, and tried to indicate sensibly.

123

'Leave it there,' said Tony. 'It'll be all right. You can come with us.'

Joe allowed himself to be led back to the black car. He was guided into the back seat and Tony got in beside him. Joe tried to see who was driving them away. It was Mac himself.

'What's up?' said Joe, trying to sound innocent, though his whole body was shaking uncontrollably.

'We've been keeping an eye on you,' said Mac lightly. 'Glad we did now.'

'You need help, Joe,' said Tony. 'It's time you saw a psychiatrist.'

CHAPTER SIX

KASSY WOKE SLOWLY FROM A DEEP SLEEP.

She found herself lying in bed, staring at some familiar clutter on the mantelpiece across the room, beyond the foot of the bed. There were some cards, the silver box she'd loved as a child, a drawing she'd made of some grasses. To her left there was the desk, and she could see the blue sky through the window. She turned her head back and looked beyond the big wicker chair at the frayed Persian carpet hanging on the wall, and followed the patterns on it with her eyes. She was back in her own bed at the flat.

At first she thought the whole episode had been a bad nightmare. She remembered the row with her father. Perhaps she'd come straight home, and dreamt the rest: the riot and Joe coming to help her. But when she tried to sit up in bed, she realised how bruised and battered she felt. She was still dressed, but her trousers were torn, and her knees bruised. Her shoulder and her left arm gave her considerable pain. It didn't seem to be a dream. At that moment Boff came in.

'Don't go near the window,' he said. 'I don't think it's safe.' Then he came carefully round and sat on the edge of the bed. He seemed unusually concerned as he said, 'You've been asleep for a couple of hours. How are you feeling?'

'What happened?' she asked. 'How did I get back here?'

'Apparently you told them where we lived. It seems we're under some sort of house arrest.'

Kassy looked nervously round the room, and then felt the horror of her own betrayal.

'Oh Boff,' she said, 'I didn't mean to get you involved.'

'It's all right, I don't mind,' said Boff, and he grinned. 'So long as they don't interrupt my work! But you've no broken bones or anything?'

She moved about the bed. 'I don't think so. I'm just bruised I think. They kept pushing me about.' She shrank back, suddenly afraid. 'Where are they now?'

Boff lowered his voice a little. 'There's two of them at the bottom of the stairs all the time and one in the street. They've taken over Danby's shop as well, as part of their HQ. I'm worried about old Mr Danby and Ginnie. I heard them being taken off somewhere, and then they smashed the shop window downstairs. But they seem to want us kept here. One of them comes up every hour or so to check us out.'

Kassy warned, 'Be careful what you say.'

'I hope you haven't got concussion or anything,' Boff went on. 'You were almost unconscious when they brought you in.'

Kassy tried to remember what had happened. 'I kept saying I was on their side. So they wanted to know who I was and where I lived. I think I might have been killed there and then, if it hadn't been for Ranji. I don't suppose you know him but he's one of Dad's –'

'Careful,' said Boff, putting a finger to his lips.

Kassy lowered her voice again, and whispered: 'They must know who our father is, so what do you think they'll do to us?'

Boff didn't answer, but looked hopelessly vulnerable, like the seven-year-old boy she used to drag away from his computer screen, to take for walks down the Backs.

There was a sudden sound of laser shots from some nearby street and the sound of shattering glass. A shout, and the sound of running feet. A stir from downstairs; alertness and tension everywhere.

'What's happening?' said Kassy.

'They're trying to take over the city. I was listening to your friend Ranji downstairs. He says they're going to attack Super-seed House, burn it to the ground. He said all this may have started like a demonstration, but it's been planned to develop into a full-scale military uprising.'

There was an urgent shout from down the street, and from the shop doorway below a man responded by running off down the road. Boff stood up and looked as if he might move towards the window, but Kassy caught his hand. Further away in the city there was an explosion, a dull thump followed by the rumble of falling brickwork. Somewhere someone was screaming.

Boff was pale as he sat on the bed again; all his natural exuberance had drained out of him. Kassy found herself crying, and once she'd started she couldn't stop. She thought of that strange vision of Joe Goodman holding out his hand to her, trying to help. But hadn't he been responsible for all this?

She didn't know if she thought of him with love or hate. The tears flowed. Boff was sitting on the edge of the bed rocking backwards and forwards as he had done as a child – lost in thought. There were more laser shots somewhere in the city, and then, from nearby, an incongruous burst of merry laughter. Kassy turned away and buried her face in the pillow. After a while, she felt Boff's hand absently patting her side.

'Don't worry,' he said.

'I feel like such a failure,' she cried. 'Everything I do seems so useless. How can I hate my own father? But I hate everything he stands for; in some ways I hope they do blow up his precious offices. They're welcome to my seed bank… But even there I'm a failure! I can't get the plants to grow. I've even tried at the cottage.'

Boff looked down at her, shocked. 'You've tried what?'

'How would you know anything? You never come down there – no one does except me. But even there they won't grow. I'd give them all to these people today, but they wouldn't be any use, that's the ironic joke. This whole business of storing the world's seeds to preserve diversity is a fraud, Boff. All we've ever done is provide a source of genes for ourselves. And now the bloody genes can't even grow into plants on their own.' She was laughing and crying at the same time.

Boff looked gently down at her. 'Kassy,' he said, 'you're being really self-destructive; do you know that?'

'Sometimes I feel like being self-destructive,' she cried aggressively. 'It's all such a failure, and I feel like tearing up the world and starting again.'

'I know,' said a quiet voice from the doorway. 'I have felt the same.'

They both looked up, startled. It was Ranji. Kassy wondered how long he'd been standing there.

Ranji came and sat down in the big wicker chair at the right-hand side of the bed. There was a long silence. Kassy stopped crying. For the first time she was really able to look at the man. He was thickset with small, almost dainty hands and feet. He seemed very sure of himself.

'My name is Ranajit,' he said.

'I know –'

'You don't know anything, little rich girl,' he returned sharply, and she froze.

'I think you may have saved my life,' she said more carefully. 'Why?'

'You may be useful to us,' he said.

'What's happening out there?' Kassy asked after a moment.

'We're consolidating our positions.' The reply was vague.

Kassy tried again. 'What will happen to us?'

'You'll be held until the final assault is over. Then we'll decide how best to use you. It seems I'm the only person who's aware of your true value. Except your father of course.'

Kassy became cold.

'I'll help in any way I can,' she said simply.

'You will,' was the simple reply.

There was another silence and she tried to work out the implications. What did they want? Perhaps they were after inside knowledge of some kind, access to the seed banks perhaps. But Ranji must know enough to know the uselessness of that. She tried to remember what conversations with her father he might have overheard. He must know that she was at least sympathetic to their cause. Perhaps he hoped to convert her completely. But no: it was far more likely that they were hoping to use the children simply as hostages, to force the father to make concessions, or for a ransom, or even as some kind of bait. If so, she knew her father would never give in to threats; he had often publicly said so. When she tried to think of where that might lead, she stopped, not daring to pursue her thoughts further.

Somewhere beyond the nearby houses, there was a rattle of laser fire.

Eventually Ranji said, 'We have some time yet. Let me tell you a little story.' His voice was magnetic, hardly more than a whisper.

'Once, in a village in Bihar, on the very edge of the Ganges plain, my father had a small farm. A few hectares. But he was a good farmer, and he prospered. You can see it was a long time ago. But all around him, his friends and neighbours were going out of business. Their farms were too small, and they got into debt. Soon he was about the only farmer left; and all around him, all the way to the horizon grew the identical crops from Superseed. They were mostly for export. The biggest land-owner locally had been chosen as the "progressive farmer", and now he had cheap loans from the city and a fleet of tractors. But my father was stubborn. He kept many animals on the farm for manure; and he knew his land well, and as a child he would take me into the fields and show me every year how to choose the best and healthiest plants to be the parent for the next year's crop. And always he'd say, "Look after the soil, and the soil will repay you." The big landowner would laugh at him, but my father was stubborn. His crops were never as good as the Superseed crops, but he sowed his own seed, and his soil was in better heart, and he sold his surplus in the village as best he could. We all fed well most of the time.

'But when I was still only a small child, came the great blight. You read of that in your father's history, I'm sure. But your history is different from the truth. Let me tell you. That year, the fields all around our farm were struck. The Superseed crop simply withered and died. But as if by a miracle, our crops were untouched by the blight and the harvest was good. And that year my mother sang a lot as she prepared the meal, and my father came back from the market with a smile on his face and a wad of money in his jacket. And I was told that I could go to school.'

Boff stirred slightly and Ranji said, 'Be patient. You will soon understand the point of my story.'

An absolute stillness fell over the room. The afternoon sun was slanting through the windows, and from her bed Kassy watched tiny dots of dust floating in the sunbeams.

'That winter, two men from the city came to visit my father. I remember it as a small child, because they were friendly and made a fuss of me. My father was very respectful to the strangers because they wore suits and came from the city, and my father was a simple man. They all sat round the kitchen table with the new red cloth on it which I loved. And I was told later what they had said. They said to him: for the good of everybody we should like to take some samples of the seed, so that we can find out why they have grown so well. Many people have starved, they said, because of the failure of so many crops, but yours seem to have done well. We would like to protect the world from starvation in the future, they said. May we take samples of your seeds? And my father said, "Yes, of course," for he had always shared his knowledge with all his friends and neighbours and was glad to be of help. So he gave them samples of his seeds. All I remember was that the men gave me a can of Supercola when they left.

'And for the next few years our family prospered and our farm did as well or better than the big landowners around us. I learnt to read and write and wanted to understand the world. My father dreamt that I should be able to go to agricultural college one day and speak to those men on equal terms. But after a few years, a new Superseed strain was introduced in the fields all around us and the blight disappeared. And now we found our produce harder and harder to sell. And then, one summer the rains failed and there was a drought and our bore-hole dried up because the big tube well on the rich farmer's land, which the Superseed company had supplied, was taking all the water from the underground water-tables. My mother and the other women of the village had to walk miles to fetch even our expensive drinking water, and our crops failed.

'That winter – it was sometime in the late '20s – some more gentlemen came from the city, and this time the big landowner came with them. This I remember well, because I was growing now and no longer thought of myself as a child. But I was still not considered old enough for such talk and I was angry. Again, my father sat with these men around the kitchen table with the old red cloth on it which I loved. And I listened outside the open door. The men told my father that he was growing plants illegally because the seeds had not been author-ised by Superseed. They said they would be generous and offer him a great deal of credit to buy a tractor and grow the new Superseed variety, and that they would guarantee to buy all his surplus produce for a good price. But my father refused. I do not want to be indebted to you, he said; I am happy as I am, and I do not trust you. Then the big landowner said to the men from the city, do you see how stubborn he is. He said to my father: I will give you enough money to leave your farm. And he offered my father a great deal of money, and I could tell that my father was tempted, because times had not been good. But he had great pride, my father, and he would not give in to them. And then they all grew angry, and the men from the city said he was acting against the patent laws and they would have to make him pay a fine; and then they drove away in their green truck. At the same time the landowner too made threats, and drove his car away in a fury. My father shouted at them all as they left. Afterwards he went to his room. It was the first and only time I ever heard my father cry.'

Ranji stopped. He was listening. The afternoon sun was hot and the stillness in the room was intense. Down in the street someone could be heard banging a nail into some wood. There was still the odd rattle of laser fire, but it seemed to be further in the distance now. All trace of self-satisfaction had left Ranji's face now and his eyes burnt large and dark.

'We had a choice,' he went on. 'We had to accept a fine, or a loan, or sell up. Whichever course we chose, we were ruined. Evil things started to happen to us. Our crops were trampled in the night. There was a fire in one of our barns. My father never really recovered. Every year the rains were less. His heart went out of farming. He took the loan, and tried to farm the Superseed way; but he hadn't enough land, and there was no doubt he was in the way of the great machines on their way from one horizon to the other, and eventually he was forced to sell out to the rich landowner. He tried to work for a while as a tenant but he was proud and unhappy and he was at last evicted. Only then did I realise how truly rich and privileged we had been. We were forced to leave our home and he left us in the hands of a relation in the bustees of Kolkata.

'There were so many people leaving the land, there were so many people dying. We lived in one room by the East Canal, while he went to look for work. He worked as a roadbuilder for Superseed for a while. His last job was as a casual labourer on a big Superseed irrigation aid scheme; but by now he was old and difficult, and in any case, once the dam was built there was no more work. He stopped sending back money and I watched my mother become the slave of another man. After they both died in the great floods, I went to look for my father. I looked for a long time. Finally, I tracked down a report of him on the streets of Delhi. They said it was something else but of course he had starved to death.'

Ranji fell silent.

Kassy saw that he was trembling, and realised he was speechless with anger. At last, he controlled himself and said, 'I have been lucky to have survived and to have found my way to England. Now I am determined to find justice.'

'From Superseed?' asked Kassy.

'Of course. Superseed killed my father. Destroyed my family. There are many others they have killed. They take the skills and knowledge of poor people for nothing and then turn them into profit for themselves. And when they do this, they don't see who they kill, and so they don't care. They take this land that our ancestors have nurtured for centuries and turn it into profit for themselves. And when, finally, they kill the land, then they kill all our children and our children's children and they don't care. This is unforgivable. This can never be forgiven.'

'But surely –' began Kassy timidly, but the anger flashed back more strongly than ever.

'If you talk of forgiveness, spare me. There are some evils that can never be forgiven. Only those who know nothing about such things could ever suggest forgiveness.'

Ranji stood, and the power of his presence filled the room.

'There is only one thing you have said which makes sense to me,' he went on. 'When you said you felt like tearing up the world and starting again. That I understood.'

And he left the room.

Laser fire echoed around the city all afternoon.

It seemed a long afternoon, and most of the time Kassy remained in bed, still in her clothes, unable to stir herself, still in a state of shock, and in some pain from her throbbing shoulder. Boff had gone back to his room, and she could hear him across the hallway muttering to himself and hitting his desk every now and then with a shout or a laugh. It was amazing how quickly he could cut himself off, disappearing into the world of his work for hours on end. Even with all this going on.

And still there were laser shots and occasional explosions.

She lay and wondered how her father would be reacting now, what terrible orders he might give. The attack would be closing in on him, and for all her sudden new hatred of everything he stood for, she couldn't help feeling fear for him. She wondered if he would have heard of her capture. Even if he knew she was a hostage, there was nothing she herself could do.

But her thoughts about her father came back to her later in the afternoon, when there was a sudden crescendo of shooting from the nearby streets. Despite herself, Kassy got out of bed and crossed to the window, her curiosity overcoming her caution. She stood beside the window and tried to glimpse out sideways. At first she could see nothing. Then some distance away, down by the traffic lights, she saw some green-uniformed police who were pinned down by fire from an upper window somewhere out of sight. Two of them were sheltering in a doorway, and another was crouching behind a builder's skip in the street. Sparks were flying from the tarmac all around the skip. Suddenly the two of them were running, across the traffic lights, and then up the street towards her. The one behind the skip remained, trying to cover them, but he was pinned down by their enemy's fire. The two men had made it to the shelter of a doorway not far down the street. Kassy waited to see what would happen.

Suddenly one of the two policemen left the shadow of their doorway and ran several doors up the street towards her. There was no response from their enemy. A moment later the other ran too, passing his friend and sheltering in a doorway still nearer to her. They were leapfrogging up the street towards Kassy and Boff's place, and Kassy's heart was suddenly full of misgiving. There was a deathly silence from down below. Were they coming to rescue her, these policemen? Would her father have given or approved such orders? All that could be heard now was the sudden clatter of boots when the men in uniforms made a dash for a closer doorway. Kassy watched, as best she could, mesmerised by the scene, and the uncanny stillness that lay behind it.

Then at the last moment, just as the two green uniforms ran together to reach the door of the shop below, somebody whom Kassy couldn't see stepped out from the same door downstairs and the shattering burst of a stream-laser screamed down the street. In an instant both men were stopped in their tracks, on their faces a look no more complicated than surprise. They seemed to step forward again for a moment, then another stream of fire swept them backwards, knocking them over. One of their faces split open and half a head seemed to disappear down the street in a streak of red and white.

Kassy turned from the window and went to be sick in the bathroom. She knelt by the pan, locked in a nightmare. This had been no 'dispensable' extra in a video film, but a real man whose death, so seemingly accidental, could shatter the lives of others all around him. His wife. A favourite child. She was shocked by the utterly casual nature of the end of life, against which we try so pathetically to build comfort and safety.

Later she glimpsed into Boff's room, where he sat, an odd figure in front of the screen, in total absorption, working on some strange and complicated shapes. She couldn't bring herself to say anything to him. There was more firing and shouts from outside. She thought she could hear Ranji downstairs, talking on a mobile phone. He seemed to be giving some orders. She crawled unsteadily into bed again.

Afternoon moved into evening and the firing moved away, and rumbled round the town like distant thunder. She dozed.

And she dreamed.

She didn't know what creature she had become. She only knew she was drowning in a sea of blood. The cold black and red

137

waters were all around her and she was sinking into the darkness. She could just see the lighter green of the surface waters above her, but she was sinking, and the light was becoming dimmer and dimmer. And she knew she would soon be dead.

And then with a sharp click or 'ping', a beautiful warm shape opened in her mind, full of colour and light, moving with a rich complexity, dancing with a majestic music. She felt utterly safe, a warmth beyond death. She found herself turning towards the source of the colour and shape as you might turn towards a light behind you, turning inwards to it, sharpening its focus in her mind. Then with a sensuous, powerful flip of her whole being, like the crack of a whiplash, she moved forwards, feeling her way through the deep towards the source of light. And she knew that she was answering a call, and that the call was from Joe.

Suddenly the colours and sounds were forming in her own mind without her searching for them, so that even as she woke, she was sending back an answer, which shot forth into the darkness in front of her, reaching forwards – or was it backwards – into the depths of time.

There is a space in a cetacean's head like a cave, where sound waves concentrate, laser-like, into intentions of such power that one lazy tap can stun a giant squid for food, or softly flick a message through a whole ocean in the search for love.

Incoming raw sound is translated into video-acoustic pictures on an acoustic retina, almost like a screen. What pictures are playing now on that acoustic screen are beyond the under-standing of man. But worthy of respect. A massive intuitional intelligence is at work, a cooperative mind developed over fifty million years. And now it is sensing a sudden changing of the seas, and is puzzling about the destructive urge of this recent new species, somewhere out to land. It is reading the warmth of poison, the spread of algae blooms, the death of coral, the storms that suck up the whirling water high above. It is reading the fear in the ether. Its mind is moving beyond the usual concern for individual life and death. Now it must be concerned with the death of a whole species – be it whale or man – and the chance of survival afterwards.

Urgency is hard for a mind that prefers to joke and play among the many dimensions of space and time, and that thinks in spans of centuries; but the game is up now. Now, intuitional probes into the future meet only a great oncoming darkness. Time is leaking away fast.

Only a short cut will serve.

When Kassy woke from the confusing remnants of her dream, it was getting dark. Ranji was standing over her bed, looking down at her. As she started back in fright, she sensed also how painful her shoulder had become.

'You've no need to be frightened,' he said, and at once turned to put a book back on the bookshelves at the head of her bed. It was the first of her father's Superseed history books.

'Read it if you want,' she said.

'Propaganda,' he said. 'For the rich of the cities. Like so many books. I don't need to read it.' He abruptly left the room.

The light outside the window had almost faded and there seemed to be an unnatural hush all over the city. She eased herself out of bed and, cautiously crossing the space, she approached the window. Taking great care, she forced herself to glance out from the shadow of the curtains, but the street was bare. There were bloodstains in the middle of the street, but that was all that remained. The bodies had been dragged somewhere. The only sound anywhere was the lazy tap of Boff's keyboard from the other room; and the occasional explosive noises he made to urge himself onwards.

She felt hungry and made her way to the kitchen to make a sandwich. She was lucky to find the last of a precious loaf hidden in a cupboard, and some cheeses. As she steadied herself on the sideboard, to cut the bread, an acute pain shot through her arm and shoulder. She came back into her room with two cheese sandwiches on a plate, and stood, feeling lost; the silence was uncanny. On an impulse, she picked up the first volume of the Superseed books and went through to Boff's room. She put down the plate beside Boff and then took one of the sandwiches unsteadily to the old sofa in the inner depths of the room and sat there. Boff hardly stirred.

'How can you go on doing that, in the middle of a revolution?' she asked him.

'Because I'm on the verge of a breakthrough,' he said absently, 'which will make all the revolutions in history seem very unimportant.' He tapped away for a while, and a complicated series of equations came up on the screen. He murmured, 'The verge of a breakthrough...' again, and sighed. 'Or the edge of a breakdown...' he said, and laughed.

Kassy opened the book to the chapter entitled 'The Technical Breakthrough'. Yet she dreaded reading about Joe. It would surely be propaganda. So she said:

'I found out who the man was in my dream, Boff.'

'Who?' he said, absent-mindedly, never taking this eyes off the screen.

'Joe Goodman.'

Boff turned towards her, his face suddenly alive with interest. 'What?' he said.

'Joe Goodman. You know, the inventor of the first Superseed.' She dropped her voice almost to a whisper. 'There's a picture of him in Daddy's office. I suppose that's where I got it from.'

Boff's switch of attention was now total; it seemed to relate to something he was already thinking. It only took him a few seconds to link into the library on his PC where he asked for the 'history of science' section of the encyclopaedia. He soon came up with a potted history of Joe Goodman's career, and then a photograph. He was an eminent, white-haired man like the portrait in her father's room.

'Good God, you're right,' said Boff. 'It's the same man. Hey, where's your dream card got to?' As he rummaged about for it, Kassy took it out of her pocket and held it out to him.

'Are you sure you don't mind?' he said, suddenly embarrassed. She shrugged, so Boff took it and put it eagerly into his PC. Then he took the two images of Joe, superimposed them, and then mixed them, sliding back and forth from one image to the other.

'Only in your dream he's still a young man. How old, would you say? 30? So why is that? Let's look at the dates.'

Kassy started to look up the date chart at the back of her father's book, but Boff was there first on the computer.

'Here we are. Born… er… discovered Superseed… er… yes, he must have been about 31 or 32. You've dreamt of him just at the time he put together his first Superseed discovery! Why just then…? Wow! I wonder if we could use this…'

His fingers were flailing all over the keyboard. Kassy couldn't understand the symbols which covered the screen, or the changing shapes which were representations of four or more dimensions. Boff was silent for a long time, while Kassy ate her sandwich. His concentration was intense. Finally he turned to her.

'Kass…' he said, 'have you had other dreams about him since?'

Kassy hesitated. She felt wary of telling him about her waking dreams; she would seem crazy; and yet she had no one to help her understand herself except Boff.

'You'll think I'm mad,' she began, and then she told him of the strange intuitions she had experienced. An antique car following hers; a vision of him digging in the field; holding out his hand to her in the midst of her terror. The only moment she somehow couldn't tell him about was their meeting on the landing at the cottage. She was still afraid of his brotherly laughter and scorn.

But Boff wasn't laughing. He listened to her in silence, occasionally rising from his seat in a paroxysm of excitement and then taking a turn among the debris on the floor, before sitting again, his head in his hands. When she finished, he was silent for a long time. Eventually he said: 'Those are more like waking visions, or what are called "reinforced intuitions". What about dreams?'

She told him the dream of entering the water. And then added, 'Oh, and just now I dreamt we were both whales, trying to reach each other across the ocean.'

Boff exploded with what seemed for a moment like laughter. But so many different thoughts and feelings seemed to be crossing his face at once that she didn't know what to make of it.

'Yes, yes, yes!' he said at last and loped about the room for a bit. 'If only I had a card of that... If only...' Then he said abruptly, 'Yes of course, here in the same labs, the same place as you. You have the same background, the same areas of knowledge. It all fits. No wonder...'

Suddenly he stopped speculating, and swung his chair round to face her. 'Kassy,' he said seriously, 'it is possible that this is just a dream world of yours. No particular meaning. You're upset by your powerlessness and you're looking around for help, for some kind of guidance.' He flung out an arm in an odd gesture.

'But it is also just possible that these encounters have an objective existence and that help is really on its way. If so, Joe Goodman will also be thinking of you. He knows you're in the future and is trying to get through to you. I think we should go on that premise. Then, if we record your dreams, and analyse and reinforce them, I really believe we could engineer a singularity in space-time. Don't you see, if he could communicate to us – just one useful piece of knowledge – then perhaps, with his brain, and at the height of his powers, he could give us the key piece of information we need to see us out of the mess we're in.'

Kassy could see now which way Boff's mind was working. He wanted to use Joe, to use his mind to engineer a technical fix to the Superseed crisis. Something in her rebelled against the idea...

'No,' she said. 'I don't believe he wants to teach us anything.'

Boff stopped and looked at her strangely.

She tried to explain. 'I think he's looking for answers as much as we are.'

'What makes you say that?'

She couldn't say, she couldn't explain. She suddenly regretted not having kept her world secret. She thought how easily distorted and crushed our subtle intuitions are, by another's perception of them.

'What are you thinking?' said Boff.

Kassy felt confused again. 'I only know there's something important there, but I don't know what it is.'

'And do you think he feels that too?'

It was a moment before she answered.

'Yes,' she said.

'Then at least you agree we must try to maximise the chances of communication.' He was excited again. 'He won't know from the state of knowledge of half a century ago, how close that possibility could be. So it's really up to us to get the conditions right. We must –'

'Boff…?'

She half wanted to stop him. Something in all this she hated. It was as if she had put herself into the hands of an overeager matchmaker. And she didn't even know what she felt about Joe Goodman.

But he swept on: 'Don't you want to find an answer to all this chaos?' he asked.

'Oh Boff, of course I do. Why do you think I've been dreaming of nothing but starvation for months? Of course I do.'

'Then why shouldn't we use Joe Goodman to help us?'

'I've told you – I don't think a technical solution is the answer.'

'But does he?'

'I don't know!' she cried in anguish.

'Then why don't we find out?' he cried passionately in response.

There was a long silence.

'Go on,' she said, defeated.

And so she tried to take in Boff's description of the latest research on how two beings' thoughts might connect across an ocean at the same time; or across an interval of years in the same place. In either case making the connection seemed to depend on a specific 'resonance' in thought patterns. The technique was to monitor the brain and then mirror the result on a neural network parallel processor for analysis and adaptation. If the 'resonances' were powerful enough it could in theory then pull space and time together in a 'singularity'. As Boff explained all this, he was punching up a whole lot of mathematical equations and illustrations on the screen, so fast that Kassy was soon left behind.

'Oh sorry,' he said at last, 'I keep forgetting you didn't do all this multi-dimensional stuff at university.'

'I did agriculture,' said Kassy, 'very little maths. And only six months' cross-discipline.'

'Oh God!' said Boff in disgust. 'But trust me. It all works. I've decided you just need to realise images in conditions where there are as few variables as possible, record them and reinforce them. Realise, record, reinforce. The three Rs. I'm coming to the conclusion that to cross time at a singularity you must be feeling strongly along the same lines. I suspect you two both want to communicate quite badly or you wouldn't feel as you do. But the other problem is, if you want to cross time, you need to be in the same space. So the only remaining question is where to meet?'

'The cottage,' said Kassy at once.

Boff looked glum.

'The trouble with that is that it's miles out of Cambridge. And it's going to be hard enough to get out of here at all in the present circumstances.'

They both suddenly fell silent, and listened. Outside in the city, it was still very quiet, but the atmosphere was charged with an expectant tension. Downstairs they could hear quiet voices; and again Ranji was talking on the mobile phone.

'Where then?' asked Kassy, half reluctantly.

Boff's face lit up. 'How about the labs?' he said. 'That has to be the place to exchange knowledge. You must both have worked there for years of your life, in exactly the same place. They're very old labs. If you don't count the new extension, and the seed-cloning factory at the back, they must be very similar physically, then and now.'

Kassy thought about it. It had to be true. They were known as the Goodman labs, though she'd rather taken it for granted before. She felt strangely torn: part of her excited, part distrustful.

'Mind you,' said Boff, 'it's easier said than done. You've got to get out of here first.' He paused thoughtfully. 'I must tell you though, even if you do, there's one problem with a singularity. The mathematics imply that it could work one of two ways. It could result in a physical meeting, or transfer, either from past to future, or from future to past. From him to you could work well; on the whole it seems it would be safer for us, because our future has not yet been chosen, and what lies between him and us need not be affected much. On the other hand, transferring anything at all from the future into the past could have much more drastic effects, as it could change the whole world in between; it could collapse the world into the whole new reality of some parallel world, with unpredictable results. It might be only a slightly different world; or it might be vastly different. But the transfer would certainly behave chaotically and be very difficult to predict...'

Kassy could guess the way Boff was thinking, and she didn't like it.

'So you see, it would be much safer if the impetus came from him and not you. If we can assume that he knows the future is in trouble and if we can make the connection for him, then he may succeed. He may be able to transfer to us at least some kind of suggestion – some specific gene perhaps which might work with the present Superseed gene to save it from the plague.' Boff was starting to get excited again. 'Yes!' he said. 'That's brilliant! That's it!'

Something seemed to snap in Kassy's mind and she felt a cold fury rise in her.

'No,' she said. 'It might be safer if he realises he should never have invented a Superseed in the first place.'

'That's just negative, Kassy,' said Boff, flinging up his hands. 'Destructive.'

'Is it?' she said. 'What has Superseed done for the world except made the poor more and more dependent on our technology, till now they're starving? Ranji is right, it's taken away all our dignity. Even I can understand that. What am I doing? I pretend to be preserving diversity for them in my bloody seed bank but it's a farce. A farce.' Now she took herself by surprise by the violence of her own anger. 'There wouldn't need to be seed banks if diversity had really been respected; if we could grow and eat our own crops without interference. At least we could starve in our own way. But Superseed isn't there for any of us, is it; it's there to make profits and keep power. It's time Joe Goodman saw the danger and took a different course.'

Boff looked at his sister with surprise. He'd never seen her so angry. 'Kassy, you're crazy.'

There was a long silence.

Boff repeated, more quietly and with his voice sounding strange: 'You're crazy.'

At length Kassy answered.

'Perhaps,' she said. She felt desperately tired, and her left shoulder was throbbing painfully.

'Excuse me,' said Ranji softly from the doorway. 'I've just come to say that we now hold almost all of the city.'

How long had he been standing there? Neither of them had heard him come in. Boff scuttled back to his computer screen like a guilty schoolboy caught away from his desk.

'The final assault on Superseed House will begin shortly.'

Kassy's thoughts returned to her father, probably besieged in his penthouse, surrounded by an army of 'dispensable' green uniforms. She could almost feel his icy, outward calm, his seething inward panic. And she didn't know what she felt. If he knew they were holding her, would it make any difference to his judgement as to whether to fight or surrender? What would happen to him?

She opened her mouth to speak to Ranji, but he cut her off. 'As for your father,' he said, as if he had heard her thoughts, 'I don't know what will become of him. But you will remain here until it's over. Then we shall have more time to decide about you. I promise you I'm prepared to take the hardest decisions about you if I must. I don't trust you, and if I have to, I shall kill you.' Then he added more gently, 'It's late. Go to sleep now. In the morning, one way or another, you will have all the answers you need.' He seemed tense and distressed as he left.

Kassy and Boff looked at each other and shrugged.

'It's sleep then,' she said.

'Kassy…' began Boff. He looked apologetic, and clearly had something more to say. 'Kassy, will you let me monitor your dreams tonight? It might be useful, to interpret things, so we can start to get the conditions right. But it's up to you.' He seemed needy.

Kassy felt reluctant. Dreams were so wayward and unpredictable, and she didn't altogether trust Boff not to use his knowledge of her for his own research ends. It was just another 'technical fix'. She felt tired and pressured, unable to think straight. But finally she agreed, and Boff helped her take the dreamcorder with her when she went to her room. She set it up on the wide bookshelves behind her bed, angling it down towards her pillow, adjusting it carefully.

She shut the door of her room, but she didn't dare undress: she took off only her shoes and got into bed with her clothes on. She lay and forced herself to read for a little, the chapter about Joe Goodman. There again was the story her father had

149

told at the meeting last week, how Joe Goodman had disappeared for a while before releasing his research. Then he'd published in *Nature* and there'd been a series of big press conferences. It had really caught the public imagination. There was a photo in the book from one such conference; Joe was smiling happily. He joined Superseed as soon as it was set up. He was still quite young. He became their Chief Scientist. Married someone called Sarah. They had four children.

A wave of exhaustion came over her. She closed the book, put on the dreamcorder and turned off the light. Her thoughts went from Joe to the present crisis and the starving and the fighting; and then she was listening for sounds in the street. She was troubled by the image of the man shot in the street, with his brains blown away. Had she seen, or did she just imagine, the body dropping sideways into the road, blood pumping from the stump of his neck? It was so silent outside now. She couldn't remember what had happened to the other man. Perhaps he'd just sort of folded up like crumpled paper and burnt.

She lay in the dark for a long time, thinking. She thought of the fear which made her father vicious, and Boff's single-mindedness; and then of her long-suffering mother, and days of childhood by the sea. 'Give us this day our daily bread…!' She felt afraid and longed to be safe.

Finally she settled down, slipping slowly as if into a deep water, dropping down to sleep.

But her sleep was dreamless. Her mind was utterly black and dark. For hours and hours. Almost out of time. And yet all this while she seemed to be rolling slowly forward through the dark. Until slowly she became aware of a point of light a great distance away. It was moving towards her, or was she moving towards it? A glowing point of light that suddenly accelerated towards her, spread across her mind, exploding into bright shapes and colours, opening like a sea flower with a sharp music. But this time the sense of it was different. It was a shattering cry for help; an urgent and imperative summons. Faster it cried, faster. She responded instinctively and at once, feeling the resonance, feeling the response of her whole body, rolling forward, driving faster through the water, surging through the darkness, till she was racing in reply, shifting the whole weight of time in the passionate desire to reach him, and always projecting a message before her as she moved: I really am on my way now Joe, I am coming with an answer, I am coming, I am coming…

And when she woke she was crying.

CHAPTER SEVEN

.JOE LAY BACK IN ONE OF MR DAVITSKY'S ARMCHAIRS, while the man painstakingly explored the meaning of Joe's 'cry for help'. He made him go through all his dreams and hallucinations very carefully. It seemed to take hours and the afternoon was passing very slowly. Joe felt he was talking all the time.

Outside he could see the sun on the stone walls of Peterhouse across the street. It had been a hot, still afternoon, though Mr Davitsky's room was cool enough. It was slightly old-fashioned, full of dark wooden bookcases and with a polished dining table.

'Let's go back to your original dream,' Mr Davitsky was saying now, as he paced quietly up and down the Persian carpet in the centre of the room. 'Often the first dream is the most significant.'

So Joe retold the dream of the balloons springing up, the podium, the fires and the desert, the appearance of the girl.

'Now,' said Mr Davitsky at last, 'What do you expect me to make of all this?'

'I don't know,' said Joe, rather hoping that Mr Davitsky would tell him.

'You're an intelligent man. What do you think?'

Suddenly Mr Davitsky seemed to Joe everybody's idea of the probing psychiatrist. All he needed, thought Joe, was a beard and glasses, behind which his narrow eyes could hide. The accent was just right.

'Well,' said Joe, rather nervously, 'I suppose it means I'm in a complete state of doubt and horror over what I've done.'

'What have you done?'

'I've finished my research.'

'What does this research mean to you?'

'Well, finishing it is like a party, with balloons. But I'm frightened that it will all evaporate into the desert sands, that it won't come to any good – there'll be fire and destruction. Somehow the fact that it will be a disaster is tied in with the girl in my dream, crying. Just when everyone thinks I'm such a success.'

'What does the girl represent for you, do you think?'

Mr Davitsky stopped pacing, and there was a long silence.

'I don't know,' said Joe at last. 'But she's somehow important.'

'Have you any idea what was down in that hole in the ground into which she was looking?'

Joe thought.

'No, no idea at all.' There was a pause. 'It was something to do with loss.'

'Who had lost what?'

'She had lost...' Joe was straining now... 'We had both lost...'

'Lost what?'

He could think no further. 'Something to do with the future,' he said. There was a long pause. Suddenly Joe thought illogically of the money this silence was costing the firm. Or was the company psychologist on a company salary?

'Fine,' said Mr Davitsky, as if in response to Joe's thought, and bringing the pause to an abrupt end. 'Good. And the day after that first dream, you have a hallucination of a girl in a red car. Were you aware that she was not in fact a real girl?'

'Not at the time.'

'At the time you thought she was real. What do you associate with the colour red?'

Joe sighed. This was boring. 'Danger?'

'Fine. Good. And she packed some seeds in the back of her car, and drove off. Seeds, I presume we can again take to be symbols of the future?'

This slightly annoyed Joe. 'If you insist,' he said, 'but I'm dealing with real seeds every day of the week, or writing about them. They're just seeds to me, I don't think of them as symbols of anything in particular beyond what they are. I just thought she was packing seeds in the back of her car. But if you insist.'

'I insist on nothing,' said Mr Davitsky, with a psychologist's tact. 'At the moment I can only suggest. If you agree, then we're getting somewhere. If you disagree very strongly, then, too, we may be getting somewhere.'

I'll punch your silly face in, in a moment, thought Joe, but kept silent. He was really very grateful that Mr Davitsky was taking the trouble.

'But you have said that in some way you associate this girl with the future. Your future? Or the future of your research? Or the future of everybody? Take your time.'

Joe took his time.

'All of them,' he said at last.

'And you followed her red car to the cottage, which you later hired as a means of escape from the pressures of your research.'

'Yes,' said Joe.

'And in the cottage you found yourself increasingly dreaming of her. Would you think of her as the archetypal "woman of your dreams"?'

'I don't know,' said Joe irritated again. 'She was like... herself... not like anyone else.'

'How would you describe your feelings for her...? Take your time.'

Joe took his time again.

'It's like an intuition... that it's important to get to know her more closely... that she holds some answers for me.'

'But at the same time you recognise that this girl is only a dream or a hallucination.'

There was a pause.

'I don't know,' said Joe. He must think I'm absolutely crazy, he thought.

As if in confirmation, Davitsky gave a deep sigh. Or perhaps he has problems of his own, thought Joe.

'And finally, on the way back to town you have this strange hallucination. A red balloon, which repeats your friend's phrase, is burnt. Demonstrators chant: down with your research. The girl is set upon by the crowd and you are drawn to help her. What do you make of this?'

'I suppose I'm afraid of some future disaster – that my research could be misused. And I want to help to stop it from happening.'

'Ah.' Davitsky thought about this. 'Fine. Good. Very good. And so, this is where we have reached.' He put the tips of his fingers together, as if in prayer, and put them to his mouth.

The man's an idiot, thought Joe; and then he said:

'Well yes, except there's one dream I've left out. Which I dreamt this afternoon…'

'Yes?'

Oh dear, thought Joe, this really does it. 'Well,' he said, 'I dreamt that I was sharing the mind of a whale, and that I was sending out signals to the girl, and that she was a whale too, and I was calling for her help. And we were swimming across the ocean to meet each other.'

Mr Davitsky's narrow eyes widened at this.

'Fine,' he said, restraining himself admirably, Joe thought. 'Good. Do you have any particular associations with whales, as you said you did with balloons, and the party, and the film of *Fantasia*?'

Joe thought. 'None that I can remember,' he said. 'I haven't thought about whales for years.'

There was another long silence.

'None whatsoever,' he repeated. Then, for a second, he seemed to remember some gangly Greenpeace student talking about whales at the party, but he let it go. Mr Davitsky was clearing his throat.

'Let us return to the girl, the other "whale" as it were. You have described yourself as inclined to be obsessive. Would you describe what you feel for her in this way? Or perhaps not?'

'If you want to know what I'm really obsessed by,' Joe said slowly, 'it's this. I don't like what I've done. I don't like it.' Suddenly he felt angry. 'I want to get rid of my research, burn down the labs, in fact completely destroy everything I've worked for over the last ten years. Not because it's bad research – I know how good it is – but because I'm convinced it's going to be misused. Completely misused.'

Joe was sweating. He felt violent. Even Mr Davitsky seemed a bit put out.

'Fine. Good,' said Mr Davitsky.

Then he looked at his watch. He was about to make a decision of some kind.

'I'm going to put something to you,' he said, perching casually on the dining table, 'because we're friends. And you're entirely free to accept or reject the notion. Of course. You're a highly intelligent man and I want to share my thoughts with you. I just want to know what *you* make of my thinking on this.'

He paused.

'I want to suggest that the girl represents the important figure of the "anima". Now this, as you know, can be both a positive and a negative influence in a man's life. She represents the feminine side of a man's personality. She can act as a guide towards a more rounded personality. She can draw a man away from concentrating too much on one side of himself, and show him there are other sides, which may bring him more into balance with himself. These may be prophetic insights, a greater capacity for personal love, receptivity to the irrational and so forth. She can represent the growth of his spirit…

'But also the anima may, in certain circumstances, have a negative side. This is represented in the old Greek tales of the sirens. This aspect may lead him to insecurity, to self-criticism, and perhaps to follow a dream beyond his powers of attainment. He may see her, as it were, on an island, towards which he must swim, and where he may receive the greatest joy he has ever known. He is perhaps drawn by a vision of her beauty or by the tempting song that she sings or even by her loneliness. But she will never leave her island for anyone. So he has to cross dark and forbidden waters to reach her, and in those waters he will surely drown. This figure can only lure him to destruction.

'Now I would suggest that you have created in your dreams, and your imagination, a world of the future into which this anima figure draws you. In this future lurks a terrible destruction. In this future you play out the shadow side of your personality, the dark guilt over what you might have done, the consequent nemesis for the hubris of your inventive mind. And to this destruction your anima inevitably draws you, like a siren of old. Come, she seems to say, come and see, your work is nothing, it will only lead to disaster. If it is meant to feed the world, it will lead to starvation; if it is meant to lead to diversity, it will lead to monoculture; if it points to democracy, it will lead to dictatorship. It is symptomatic of this process that as you get drawn more deeply into this world, terrorists and violence appear more frequently.

'Your unconscious mind has created this complete shadow side to your positive achievements, to denigrate them, till you become obsessed with destroying your own creativity. The temptation is acute. You not only dream, you have waking hallucinations too. The siren, here, is drawing you to destruction.'

Joe sat with his mouth open, taking this in. It all seemed so possible. He stared out of the window at the lengthening shadows on the stone wall across the street.

'But now,' said Mr Davitsky, 'let me put another possibility to you. If I may?'

'Go on,' said Joe, feeling suddenly rather tired.

Mr Davitsky smiled. He came to sit in a chair near Joe.

'You are quite simply very, very tired. After many months of single-minded work, you have reached a stage of total exhaustion. Of course those sides of yourself which you have neglected, they are ready to rear their heads. The negative anima is lying in wait. But it is not serious. You have reached a summit; a pinnacle of great achievement. You have been involved in a sustained burst of genuine creative energy for a long time. Now, you have a reaction. Of course. It is obvious. You are tired. You are simply very, very tired.'

Joe felt his eyes closing, almost as if he were being hypnotised.

'Very tired,' Mr Davitsky went on. 'Perhaps all you have experienced with this dream-girl and this "intuition" of disaster is simply a reaction, a shadow, a hallucination. The reality is the great achievement. Everything else is a dream... But you need time to take it all in. Time to rest, to restore yourself to normality.'

'Yes?' said Joe.

'May I make a suggestion?'

'Of course,' said Joe. What a fine man, he was thinking now.

'You need complete rest and relaxation for a few days, perhaps a week or two. I'm going to suggest, with your permission, and only your permission, that you go to this hospital, into a private room at the company's expense, and have complete rest until your sense of balance is restored to you…' He was scribbling on a piece of paper like a doctor. 'Only for a few days, until you feel ready to come out. Stay under observation, and just rest. Will you do this?'

'Yes,' said Joe, meekly. 'I'll do that.'

'Fine. Good,' said Mr Davitsky and smiled.

As Joe stood up to go, some strange rebellion still flashed through his mind. Who was paying Mr Davitsky, he asked himself? And the answer came back: not he, but the company. His bosses.

But in the hospital the expected routine subdued him. He checked in at reception and it seemed they already knew he was coming. He was then taken up in the lift and shown a particular room, just off a long ward. There was a bed and a basin and white walls. There were some cartoon characters stuck on the windows, Roger Rabbit and Mickey Mouse – perhaps the room had been used before by a sick child. There was also a rainforest poster, and one with mythical beasts on it, with a phoenix in the middle. He explained that he had brought nothing with him, and he was given a long hospital gown, and told that a friend would bring some of his things from his flat. He guessed that this friend would probably be Tony. There seemed to be a sister or nurse in charge, who had the best sort of no-nonsense kindness. In his room there were big windows looking out over the city. He was quite high up and could see a long way, a lot of sky. It was nearly evening, so he found himself getting into bed. He lay there, and after a while supper came. It was mince and potatoes. The nurse offered to bring him any books that he wanted to read. He was brought a selection. He found himself choosing some simple undemanding love stories, detective thrillers of the simplest kind, Agatha Christie, books he had always scorned. He had a radio above his bed. He neglected Radio 3 and 4 and chose a lot of local radio. He seemed to hear the same music over and over again. It meant nothing to him. He tried hard to stop thinking altogether. He could do without the pain. There were phone-ins every now and then, but people sometimes became obsessive about all kinds of things from housework to politics; all attempts, he supposed, to deal with loneliness. He turned the radio off then, and stared out of the window. The sky moved in the familiar chaotic cloud-shapes. Sometimes he thought of Kassy, but he tried to avoid thoughts of that kind. The name Kassy itself seemed hurtful. Kassandra, the prophet of doom. Greek, like the sirens. He tried to put it out of his mind. The nurses changed every now and then. They came round to check him, and he smiled politely at them. He seemed to sleep a great deal. He almost lost sight of night and day.

And sometimes, inevitably, he dreamt. Nothing much. Darkness mostly. Swimming in the sea sometimes. Playing in the foam. Sinking, sadly, into deep water. Nothing significant, at any rate. But then in one moment, one evening or whatever, in a flash he knew that it was all nonsense, that what he was doing was all nonsense, that he was alive, not dying, that he was moving through the water, gliding towards her, to find her. Of course his mind had closed down, of course it had, but that was only to give him more strength, just so he could conserve the strength, so he could move faster, ever faster, through the water; till he was racing through the water to find her.

And sometimes, at one point or another, Tony came to see him. He had brought him various things to put in his locker; Joe wasn't very interested. Joe was lying in bed, staring in front of him. He hadn't even bothered to get up, to get into a dressing gown. Had it been several days? He just lay, conserving his strength, for his secret inner life. His outer life had become misty: platitudes to nurses, radio jingles, occasional meals on trays. Who was paying for all this? The company, of course. He felt flattered; and yet a little part of him was amused, felt as if he was fooling them.

Tony was standing by the bed.

'Hello,' he said, and he looked really concerned. 'I've been told not to stay too long. We're told you're suffering from exhaustion. I'm not surprised. In a way it's a relief to know what the problem is, don't you think? Mac says we should keep it in the family, so no one will worry. You'll feel much better after a good rest. Still… I must say you do look a bit rough.'

'I'm fine,' said Joe and smiled. 'What are you here for?'

'Just to see how you are, me old mate. And to say goodbye. I'm off to Cairo tomorrow evening. Off on my lightning tour. Spread the word. Share the secrets.'

'Oh yes,' said Joe lifelessly.

'Bet you wish you were coming. You know, I think I'll tell the doctor…' He lowered his voice to a whisper as if he were afraid of being overheard. 'There's nothing wrong with you that a good bonk in Cairo wouldn't cure.'

'I expect so,' said Joe, smiling. 'How's Carol?'

'She's fine; sends her love,' said Tony blithely, and then added, very casually, 'Oh, by the way, Joe. Mac asked me to ask you where you've locked up your research.'

'I expect he's getting quite anxious,' said Joe, and could feel himself smiling even more.

'He really wants it,' said Tony seriously. 'And so do I, if it's not altogether too late. A few details and even a few seed samples perhaps? Just to please the natives. And I could take it in to be published for you! It all needs doing. What do you say?'

'No,' said Joe, but without conviction. Somehow it didn't seem very important to him any more.

'Where have you put it then?' said Tony, sensing weakness.

'I've locked it at the back of one of the filing cabinets,' said Joe.

'Where? In the labs?' Joe didn't answer. 'Have you got the key?'

'Somewhere. In my...'

Tony was already feeling through the pockets of the trousers crushed in the locker, looking for the key.

'Tony,' said Joe, 'I'm very tired. I want to sleep now.' Tony turned and looked at him. 'Don't go through my pockets, leave me some pride... Why don't you come back tomorrow, first thing, and I'll give it to you then.'

Tony looked as if he was about to argue, but then he just said, 'Promise?'

'If I'm still here...' Joe's voice sounded exhausted, even to him.

Tony laughed in a peculiar way. 'Sacred promise?'

Joe did the hand routine, though it went a bit wrong, because he wasn't responding quickly enough. 'Come back tomorrow, eh?'

Tony grinned. 'I'd better leave you to sleep. Have a good rest. See you in the morning then. First thing. Don't forget –'

he went into a bit of clowning – 'Nothing succeeds like Superseeds!'

Joe stared ahead of him.

Tony stopped and fell serious. 'Are you all right? What are you thinking?'

Joe seemed to have difficulty speaking. 'I've still got such a long way to go…'

'What?'

'An ocean to cross…'

'To get where?' said Tony.

'To the future,' said Joe and smiled.

Tony looked thunderstruck, but only for the briefest of moments. 'Don't be in too much of a hurry,' he said and went out laughing.

After Tony had gone, Joe lay back for a long while staring ahead of him, till he noticed that the room was slowly growing darker and the few clouds through the window were tinged with the purple colour of the sinking sun. He tried to read a book but the words danced; he listened to the music but it was irritating. So he lay back again on the pillow, and became motionless, staring at the white wall opposite and the warm glow on it which slowly rose up the wall and widened and diffused as the sun set. He wondered what he was doing there, lying still, almost as if he was trying to find his bearings, to sense what he should do and where he should go next, as if making slight adjustments on an onward path. He was waiting, he realised suddenly; he was waiting for something, perhaps for some kind of guidance.

A nurse came in and cheerily gave him some food and he sat up for a while and went through the motions that were expected of him. He made himself talk normally and lightly to her about night duties and patients on other wards. She had brought him some rice pudding as part of his supper and he couldn't eat it. They got into some kind of argument about it, and he found himself asking where it had come from. Out of a rice packet, the nurse suggested. He demanded to see the packet. The nurse said no. Where did the rice come from, he asked? Who had grown the rice? Where did they live? He watched himself growing upset. Who did they work for? Who had provided them with the seeds? The nurse tried to humour him but eventually tired of it.

'Nobody knows,' she said as if to a child and then laughed and left, returning no doubt to the desk in the main corridor. He lay still again, and he could hear her stirring occasionally in her seat, or moving the books on her desk. His hearing seemed acute. He could hear leaves rustling in the trees outside. He wondered if they were aspen trees. Somewhere at the other side of the city a bell began to toll. The time went slowly by and lights went on in the corridor outside. A dim blue light came on in his room and the sky outside the window settled slowly into night. Time seemed to be slowing as if moving more and more slowly past him, and yet filling up the space, till it seemed to be bursting.

Then all of a sudden a huge, vivid shock spread warm across his mind, a sense of Kassy, a sense of another close and equal presence more vivid than he had ever felt it in his life, either in love or in the sharp presence of loss.

Kassy was no illusion: she physically lived in an actual future, and he knew with an absolute certainty that it was at least possible for them to meet. They were heading towards some

165

kind of connection above and beyond the restrictions of time, sharing a song that was already weaving sound, like an intricate pattern on a magic carpet, that could lift them clear. In that song was a sharp desire and a great promise. He must try to get there. He must join her. An ocean of time need be no barrier.

Only then did he realise how violent was the speed with which he was racing towards her.

And somehow it came into his mind, exactly what he should do next.

*

Kassy lay in bed, her eyes suddenly wide. She had stopped crying. Her bedroom was in darkness apart from the street lamps across the road which shone yellow on the carpet that hung like a tapestry from the wall of her room. She had closed her door but light also came from the crack under it. She imagined that across the landing Boff was still in front of his computer, playing back the ancient communications of whales, or weighing up the possibilities of time travel, and she felt sorry for him. She felt as if she'd suddenly left him far behind. She was quite certain now of what she must do.

She turned and took the metal card out of the dreamcorder behind her. Then she waited, wide awake, her shoulder still throbbing. It seemed a long time to wait. Would Boff work all night? He had been known to. Occasionally she heard him say 'Damn it!' or 'Beautiful!' according to how the work was going. At one point there was animated talking downstairs, and someone ran off down the street on some errand. But still she waited.

Finally Boff made a frustrated noise and turned off his screen. A few minutes later the light in Boff's room went out. Her ears picked up every sound in the darkness. There was a row downstairs over something. Two men were quarrelling about how they were to divide some bread. It sounded as if one of them had been drinking. Then, from distant streets came the dull boom of explosives, and in response, she could hear Ranji at the bottom of the stairs, giving orders on his mobile phone. There was the sound of a dog howling not many streets away. She even fancied she could hear Boff turning over. Was he asleep yet? She took her dream card with her and ventured out on to the landing. She glanced down the stairs, and could see Ranji crouching on the bottom stair, in deep concentration, talking softly but urgently into the phone. Also crouching in the open doorway to the street was a bald man with a beer bottle in his hand and a lasergun across his knees. It would be very difficult to get past them, yet somehow she would have to find a way. But now she stepped across to Boff's room and listened. His door was slightly open, and she could hear his regular breathing, so she pushed the door ajar. Like a baby, he was unlikely to wake once he had fallen into his first deep sleep. She tiptoed over to his PC, turned it on and fed the card into it.

A soft green light from the screen filled the room. Boff stirred and turned away. Quickly Kassy pushed his door shut and, turning the sound down, slipped on some earphones. She settled herself on Boff's swivel chair.

Even in its first unreinforced state, Kassy was struck by the similarities between the patterns she saw, and Boff's translations of twentieth-century whale song. And for a moment, as she took in the abstract unfolding shapes on the screen, she had a vivid sense of Joe's presence calling her, with something of the intensity with which she'd felt it before. But even before she had become properly conscious of it, it had faded and the shapes on the screen had lost their meaning for her again.

She hesitated. Should she leave this, her last dream, on computer for Boff to analyse? She didn't want to wake him now... Her fingers tapped the keys, searching for the right place to store it.

Then, quite unexpectedly, she stumbled on a list of other computers to which Boff had access. She was taken aback. It was an extraordinarily wide pattern of contacts: not only round the university, and Superseed locally, but out on the Supernet overseas, and even into Patents Police areas. She tried to get into one or two of these but was short on passwords. In some Superseed areas it seemed he had privileged access – he was a superuser. Kassy was amazed. She had always thought of Boff as a lone wolf, a completely isolated operator.

With all this time at her disposal, she thought, she should try to get through to Superseed House, where even now her father might be fighting for his life. But presumably Ranji and his men had already thought of this, because all links with HQ had been severed some hours ago. Next she tried her father's personal line direct, using her own password. A voice explained to her that this was no longer a safe route but referred her to another part of the system. She tried again, probing for connections, not daring to use her own voice, but only the keyboard.

As she softly tapped the keys, Boff stirred in his bed. She waited and he slowly settled down again. She listened for any noise from downstairs, but could hear nothing, so she returned to work.

Then, all at once, there was a message on the screen. It was from her father to Boff, and was several days old, left on some private electronic noticeboard. It read:

You've been saying you're on the verge of a solution to all our problems as long as I can remember. As far as I'm concerned, engineering an answer to this seed problem is the only important issue. Keeping you busy is a rather expensive long-shot and I won't hesitate to cut off all funds if results aren't forthcoming.

Continue to keep an eye on Kassy. I'm not happy about her. Stop her if she does anything silly.

Report as usual.

Jonas.

She read it with shock. Her instinct not to trust her brother had been right.

She looked at him. He was sleeping soundly, curled in a foetal position, sucking his long thumb like a tiny child.

She turned the computer screen off and stood absolutely still in the darkness, waiting for sight to return. So now she knew where his money and equipment came from. She didn't really blame him; his desire to continue his sort of research had swamped all other feelings. Like an addict, he would cheat or steal or spy or do almost anything to be able to carry on his studies undisturbed. And yet he'd always pretended to be so independent and to care so little what their father thought. It was sad – because Jonas would never respect those he could bully, least of all his own son.

And yet, now she thought about it, they were not so different; their masculine way of thinking was not so far apart. They both believed in engineering the answers, joy through technology. She bent and twisted her dream card, and then broke it in two and threw it into the basket under Boff's desk. In some way she felt stronger; she knew that from now on she was entirely on her own.

She crept back to the top of the stairs. Ranji was involved excitedly on the phone. Suddenly, somewhere deep in the city, there was a huge explosion which echoed back and forth between brick and concrete. The house shook and the windows rattled as if there had been an earthquake. Instinctively, Kassy stepped back and as she did so, she saw Ranji turning to look up the stairs towards her.

Had he seen her? Quickly she stepped across into her room, darted back to bed and pulled the covers over her. She lay facing the door and closed her eyes to a slit. A moment later she could hear Ranji climbing the stairs two at a time. He looked in at her for a few seconds in silence, and then crossed the landing to look at Boff. He seemed to be satisfied, because he hurried back downstairs again.

Kassy waited. Now she could hear the sound of running steps approaching down the street and a shout from below. There was another enormous explosion in the distance. This time she was almost certain it came from the direction of Superseed House. There were some feverish whispers and then a drunken voice was raised. It was quelled by a fierce word or two from Ranji and there followed another conversation on the mobile phone. The assault on Superseed House must be under way. There were more running steps in the street below, this time clattering away from them down the street.

And then suddenly there were no more sounds from down below. Kassy waited, minute after long minute. The silence downstairs deepened. Eventually she got out of bed and went again to the top of the stairs. So far as she could see, Ranji had gone. The bald young man had taken his place at the bottom of the stairs. He was sitting against the wall, a bottle in his hands, his head down, but she couldn't tell if he was asleep or not. His lasergun was lying across his lap, and it occurred to her that it might have been this boy who had killed the two policemen. Perhaps that was why he had been drinking. Everyone else from down below had presumably been needed for the assault – only the drunk had been left behind to guard them.

She went back to her room and carefully put on her shoes. As she did so, she wondered what would happen if he woke. Would he find killing her easy now, or was it possible he'd been given orders to keep her alive? She tried to remember the snatches of conversation she had overheard but could make no sense of them. She rehearsed in her mind how she might knee him in the balls or smash him over the head with his bottle. She wondered if she'd have the courage. She went to the top of the stairs.

He was slumped against the wall, half drunk and surely asleep. Beyond him, the door to the street was open. She waited on the stairs, listening while his breathing became heavier and more regular. Slowly, step by step, she lowered herself down the stairs. When she had stepped carefully over him, she made a dash as swiftly and as quietly as she could for the doorway. He stirred but he didn't wake.

As she came into the street, a glance sideways through the broken window showed her that Danby's shop had been turned upside down, looted and destroyed. As far as she could see as she ran past, the dark interior was empty of all life. She thought of Mr Danby and Ginnie. She did notice a twentieth-century 'time cube' lying among the shattered glass in the window. It was three o'clock. But she didn't notice Ranji in the shadows, watching her and talking rapidly into his mobile phone as she ran off down the street.

*

The clock in the hospital corridor said almost three o'clock. Joe, still wearing his dressing gown, but with shoes instead of slippers, crossed the wide corridor on the way to the lavatory. The no-nonsense night nurse barely looked up from her desk. Once in the lavatories he took off his dressing gown, checked the street clothes he was wearing, and slipped back into the corridor.

As quietly as he could he ran to the main lifts. It seemed an endless few minutes until the lift arrived, and he could take himself to the ground floor. He wondered how he would cope with the receptionist if she were to challenge him. He could hardly pretend to be visiting a patient at this hour. Perhaps he could pretend to be a doctor on locum. Casually, he strolled past reception and then glanced back. The woman was leaning against the wall, practically asleep. Once in the street, he broke into a run, heading north towards the city centre.

Five or ten minutes later he had reached the centre and he slowed to a brisk walk. He headed up St Andrew's Street past Woolworths and Marks and Spencer; and then he remembered, as if it was in another time, how he had walked along this street in the first euphoric moments after finishing his research. Then he had been pleased with himself and aimless; now he was angry with himself and determined.

The middle of the night-time city was quiet, apart from the distant sound of an occasional car. His footsteps clicked down the street, the echoes bouncing off the dark glass of the shop fronts, making it sound almost as if he were walking in step with someone. He passed the cinema; it seemed unlikely that they would still be playing *Fantasia*. He passed the beefburger bar which was firmly closed now in the small hours, and the memory came back to him of the man's disappointed face. The food business, he had said, it's a killer. A killer.

He pressed on over the river and up Castle Street towards the labs. By now the hospital might well have discovered that he was missing. Mac would certainly have been alerted first, and Tony would know soon enough. They would be afraid for him, and would send out search parties. He became aware of a black car turning out of a side street ahead of him and he stepped back into the shadow of a privet hedge, until the car had passed.

As he grew nearer to the labs, he found himself walking faster and faster. There was no one else about now, and the world around him seemed more and more to fade into insignificance. He felt himself concentrating in himself all his remaining force, all his fierce desire and anger. He was moving now towards an objective, his mind certain. The technology he had used was not wrong in itself, he was sure, but it had succumbed to the old temptations that had bedevilled all scientific discovery from the spinning jenny to the nuclear bomb. Who controlled the invention? Who used it, at whose expense, and to what end? And here he knew with the clarity of daylight that his discovery was compromised: through PCCI, through Mac, through Tony, through the new patent laws, through his whole life. However brilliant his discovery, the future of the Superseed as it had been set up was a bad dream. Could there be anything more evil than trying to control the food of the world for profit? But why otherwise had they worked for years on genes to do with yield and uniformity and marketability? Why not genes for nutrition and taste and suitability to particular places? He owed to the future the sacrifice of his invention, if it should cost him his life. And Kassy was his guide into that insight, and he would follow her. He could almost sense a shadowy form, moving ahead of him in the darkness. And he felt such longing. It was possible he was mad, Davitsky was right, and she was a siren, luring him to destruction; but if so, he no longer cared. He was clear. It was time to undo it all. To save the future, the present must be destroyed.

It was a warm midsummer night and the full moon was rising behind him. Somewhere in the city a clock struck the half hour. It was half past three.

He found himself running down the long straight driveway, and the labs lay ahead of him in the moonlight.

*

Kassy doubled back through the streets, taking devious ways and trying to avoid any possibility of being seen. She felt terrified of every shadowed doorway, and made slow progress. The image of the men in green blown away by laser fire was still vivid in her mind; but so also was an image of Ranji's dying father, poking about for rotting food in abandoned Superseed crates on the dumps of Delhi. The two sides of death set up by Superseed.

She found herself at the corner of Christ's. There was a stir down the street and she caught a glimpse of some men, running towards Parkside carrying laserguns. Everywhere there was a threat of violence in the air, leaving her with dread in her stomach. Somewhere, she could hear a distant chant starting up again: 'No to Superseed!' Around the corner of the stone wall, she stumbled on the figure of a man, slumped in a wooden doorway, blood around his head. She dared not wait to see if he was alive or dead, but like an animal on a different scent, she moved quickly on.

Soon after, she passed a shop in which a screen was still silently transmitting pictures to an empty street. She caught a glimpse of some pictures from Asia, taken at an agro-service station at the edge of some would-be fields, where the wind blew the useless topsoil in a whirling dust storm. The bodies of the dying spread to the horizon.

Sickened by her own cowardice in trying to find the safest route, she suddenly struck directly up Sidney Street, boldly taking the straightest way, past Superfoods and Supermarks. It was eerily deserted now. And yet, all at once she could hear footsteps shadowing her. Frightened, she waited in the doorway of the Superspud shop to check that it was safe. Perhaps someone had seen her leave Danby's and they were following her. Still unsure, she moved on, walking faster every minute, taking the shortest way towards the labs.

She could hear to her left the sound of laser fire again, and flames were rising now over the city behind her. She stopped

175

for a moment and looked back. Somewhere there, at Superseed House, her father was facing the final assault.

At that moment she heard a strange throbbing sound and instinctively stepped back into the darker shadows of a hedge in someone's front garden. There was a massive whirring roar and she looked up. It was one of the green helicopters of the Patents Police, coming from Superseed House, rising higher and higher above the town and heading off to the west. She waited. A moment later there was another; and then unmistakeably she recognised her father's greyish helicopter, protected by another following escort, all heading off towards the west. She need not have worried whether her father would fight or surrender. He had chosen to run away, leaving others to do the fighting or surrendering for him. Yet, although she despised him for it, a part of her was relieved that he was safely gone.

The removal of her father from the scene seemed to strengthen her own resolve. It gave her an unexpected sense of being empowered. Her father had gone and she had complete control over what she was doing. Now she longed to meet Joe. It crossed her mind that she could be luring someone she loved into great danger. But it would be danger for both of them, the death of the present order, the world made new.

She found herself running down the long straight driveway. Behind her a full moon was rising; and ahead of her, beside the labs, the greenhouses glittered in the moonlight.

*

In the black shadows hidden from the bright moonlight, Joe fumbled with the keys to the lab buildings, trying to unlock the doors. For a moment he had lost awareness of the dim figure of Kassy, and a new fear had come to him. What if his research were no longer in his little office upstairs; what if they had already taken it away? He burst into the building, almost in a state of panic. Inside it was cool and dark, the hallways and corridors lit only by the moonlight which permeated through the skylights from above. He didn't trouble to put on the lights, but ran up the stairs to his office. The door was open. He turned on the desk lamp and now he had to find the little key in his old jacket and then to fit it into the lock on the filing cabinet drawer where he had hidden his research. To his relief everything was still there, the file anonymously stowed away at the back of the metal drawer where he had put it.

It seemed so long ago. Briefly he flicked through the pages of his research, and for a moment a kind of nostalgia came over him. Months and months of work were laid out here. It was a fine, fresh achievement of the intellect, a work of technical brilliance; here were the detailed figures that expressed a massive technological breakthrough. But like a giant ocean-going ship, the momentum of his course could not now be quickly checked, even if he had wanted it. And he did not want it. His nostalgia was only momentary.

With a new urgency now, Joe ran back down the stairs, carrying his research file with him. He ran along the moonlit corridor and down the few steps to the labs themselves. In his haste, he crashed into the doors with his shoulder and rebounded painfully. Putting his research under his arm, he was forced to search through the keys on his key ring. A moment later he was in the lab. The moonlight flooded in from the broad skylights above.

He was trembling with haste, and the anger was rising in him now. He threw the file open and took all the research papers into his hands. Then he crumpled and tore at them like a man possessed, and with a cry of pain, hurled them violently in front of him, on to the floor of the lab.

On the wall at the end of the long room the clock stood at ten minutes to four.

*

As Kassy approached the labs, the checkpoint on the drive with its moonlit guard-box seemed deserted. The moon was surprisingly bright on the checkpoint and the shadows deep, but she could see no signs of life. She was preparing to run past, when a shape leapt up at her out of the darkness, immediately to the left of her.

The shock was so intense that she instinctively threw herself down on the ground, and curled up tight while the shape moved in on her. It was a young policeman in green who had risen up from some bushes beside her and now stood over her, pointing a lasergun to her stomach. He was young, and frightened, and ready to fire. He kept demanding a password. She tried to offer him her pass to the labs, her ID card. But every time she moved, he screamed at her in a kind of hoarse whisper. Eventually he took her pass from her, looked at it for a long time, and slowly seemed to realise who he was dealing with. If anything, this seemed to increase his terror. 'I might have killed you,' he kept saying.

When he had calmed sufficiently, she asked: 'What's happening?'

The boy seemed reluctant to answer. He was now watching down the driveway again for any signs of movement on the Huntingdon Road.

'We're waiting,' he said at last.

A short round-faced officer appeared then, who recognised her and escorted her through the perimeter fence to the doors of the lab building. He too seemed very young.

'We've been told to guard the labs,' he told her. 'But there aren't really enough of us. Most of the fighting seems to be down in the city.' He gestured. Just then there was the crackling of flame somewhere in the direction of Superseed House, and a glow spread in the sky above the trees and rooftops. She wondered if this man knew that her father had fled.

The doors of the lab building were in darkness and locked. There was clearly no one inside. She thanked the officer and then, using her keys, passed into the main building. The officer didn't question her, but went back to his position. Carefully, she locked the doors behind her.

She turned then, and ran straight along the moonlit corridor to the doors of the labs themselves. There she stood fumbling with her keys again for a moment before she discovered to her surprise that the doors were already open. She didn't turn on the light. The moonlight from the skylights above threw a grey and ghostly light on the worktops round the room, and on the barren tiers of seed trays.

On the floor she seemed to glimpse for a moment a broken file, torn folders and crumpled papers, and she knew at once what this was.

At the end of the labs the dim face of the clock stood at almost five to four.

*

Joe had moved quickly down the corridor between the growth rooms where his marked plants glowed and the tall maize grew. At the far end he turned, and started to walk back, kicking open the doors to the growth rooms and moving in to pull out the plants. He felt no euphoria now, but only anger. He had been used. And so had Carol and Anne-Marie and Jimbo and all of them. His bosses had never wanted to produce food; they'd wanted to produce profits out of others' dependence and hunger. Not consciously of course, but they'd raised rationalisation to a fine art. As he moved back up the passageway, he threw the propagators out into the corridor on either side, pulling out the plants, throwing them to the floor. He could hear the containers smashing, could feel the plants breaking underfoot. He began to sweep the plant trays off the surfaces with his arms and then he was overturning every loose table, sending everything crashing to the floor. Somewhere in the distance he could hear the insistent tone of a siren. Police or ambulance, Mac or Davitsky, he didn't care who was coming after him. He would obliterate all his work first. Destroy it as if it had never been.

He stumbled awkwardly for a moment among the broken trays. The debris of earth and plants crunched underfoot, soft stems breaking, some still glowing with their obscene artificial light. He seemed to hear a voice from somewhere deep in his head chanting 'No to Superseed!'

At last he came back to the labs; and now, through the tiers of seed trays, rather as he had seen her on that first day, he caught a glimpse of Kassy.

Kassy locked the door behind her and then turned back to the labs. She stood in the moonlight stillness for a few moments and all she could hear was the distant sound of a fire engine or an ambulance. She was almost certain now she could see the figure of Joe at the far end of the labs and knew that the work of destruction had already begun. She began to move towards him.

But there was a crash then, and without any warning, bright splinters of light were hurtling all around her. The sky seemed to be falling in on her. She flung herself down under the shadow of a table and tried to shield her head. On the misty white worktops, microscopes and boxes of slides and glass jars were jumping and smashing and flying about.

It took her a moment to realise what was happening. The lab roof was shattered, skylights falling in a waterfall of glass, sharp and silvery, bouncing in tiny moonlit fragments off the work surfaces and off the floor around her. She buried her head in her hands.

When the glass had stopped raining down she was firmly back in her own world. Her shoulder was throbbing. Her bare arms were bleeding. Joe had gone. She could hear from outside the shouts and cries of angry people. 'No to Superseed! Smash the Superseed!' There were laser shots and screams. The violence of the revolution was catching up with her.

She thought she could hear Ranji shouting above the crowd. He would not save her life again. He would be furious at her father's escape, would be coming now to take his revenge on her.

Joe came into the labs to find that Kassy, for the moment, had gone. He could see his research, crumpled and strewn on the floor, and it fuelled his anger.

He turned to the cupboards and drawers behind him, pulling at their contents and throwing them on the floor. One of Jimbo's cupboards was locked, and he fiddled with his keys for a moment, but then grew impatient and kicked the cupboard viciously, smashing it in. He searched out any duplication of his precious research, tearing it up and throwing fragments on to the growing pile on the floor. The detailed measurements of growth that Anne-Marie had kept so painstakingly for many months; the charts of DNA where the place of every gene was so carefully recorded; every piece of shared research from other labs that Carol had studied and filed; all were swept into a heap of paper on the floor. Then the nutrients and electron microscopes and ultraviolet scanners and all the delicate instruments on the working surfaces, and the storage jars and every other item of clutter, useful or not, were swept down too, in a further waterfall of glass.

With every violent movement, Joe's anger was harnessed further, till he burnt with fury, a righteous fury against the Superseed and all it might mean for the future. All around the lab the debris grew. As he worked he could hear the chanting in his head – 'No to Superseed!' – and in his head he found himself crying out passionately: This is for you Kassy, this is for you…

*

Kassy could hear, above the sounds of laser fire and screams of terror from outside, the unmistakable sound of the main doors to the lab buildings breaking open, and the cries of triumph. She was afraid her time was running out; the chanting – 'No to Superseed!' – grew in intensity and she could hear feet running down the corridor towards the lab.

But now at last she could feel Joe's presence again. There was a pile of destruction all across the lab, and she could see him now, heaping papers on the pile, calling for help. At once she ran, over the broken glass, through the sounds of hatred from outside, to the drawers along the benches, to cupboards and filing cabinets, to every place where books and papers or chemicals were kept. Anything that could be burnt. And she too worked, in piling them on the floor.

She was aware of Joe working alongside her, feeding these preparations for a bonfire. There was another crash above her and glass smashed down all around her. And in her heart she found herself rejoicing at the destruction, and she thought: This is for you Joe, this is for you…

But then she heard a thundering at the door she had just locked and she became aware that the lab doors were being battered down. And suddenly she heard the sharp high voice of Boff, more anguished than she had ever heard it, more desperate than a child in pain.

'Kassy… Kassy!'

For a moment she froze.

'I'm sorry Kassy… Are you all right?'

Was it his doing, she wondered, that they were here? Was he guilty because he had been forced by Ranji to lead them here?

'Are you all right?'

At first Joe could make no sense of the battering at the door. Then he thought, they've caught up with me, Tony and Mac and Davitsky and the staff from the hospital. He didn't stop heaping the debris on the floor, and soon began to hear the chant clearly: 'No to Superseed! Smash the Superseed!' ... and the rhythm supported him as he worked on.

He knew where there were matches, on Jimbo's shelf, and he found them. He struck one, and bent down, putting a flame to the bottom of the pile, to the paper that he recognised to be his own torn and crumpled research. He wondered what chemicals were spilt on the floor that the flame should leap into life so fiercely. The torn research curled instantly in the fire. He watched, without regret, at the destruction of his best work. He sensed Kassy watching him, and he felt only joy because now he could turn towards her fully, to share their common triumph. Was he moving into her world? Because at that moment there seemed to come an other-worldly echo of their triumph, a coarser scream of victory, as there was a splitting sound from the other end of the lab and the wooden doors burst open.

The doors sprang open throwing huge splinters of wood spinning inwards, while the men with lasers burst in, deploying themselves at the further end of the labs. There was a roar as instant laser-fire played on the wreckage all across the lab. Whatever chemicals Kassy had spilt among the debris ignited instantly and the flames leapt up everywhere, so that the men checked in terror.

Then Kassy was aware of Ranji – was it Ranji? – now standing in the shattered doorway, as he took a lasergun from the man beside him. There was to be no escape for her as there had been for her father. He looked with steady purpose at Kassy as he lifted his laser to fire down the labs towards her.

*

Joe looked across the blaze towards Kassy, as all around her the flames grew higher. For a moment she was looking down the labs at the doorway, but now she was turning back to him, as he heard beyond question a boy's voice calling out.

'Kassy… are you all right?'

But Kassy was not all right, as down the lab a fierce white stream of fire leapt towards her and suddenly the space was full of screaming.

Yet the stream of fire never reached her.

Kassy had turned to Joe across the room, equally enveloped in fire. From the destruction of his research, he had just turned towards her. Now at last, while the space they moved in was full to bursting, time was really slowing, emptying out completely. They were looking directly at each other now, with a terrible complicity, standing in the middle of a fire. Something was almost complete. They began to move towards each other, through the flame, desperate to protect each other, and yet

185

incredibly almost laughing now; reaching out towards each other as they had tried to do once before. But this time they somehow knew it would be different.

So the whales, moving through the ocean depths, know, as their long run through the lonely dark comes towards its end, that at last there can be no error. The subtle foreplay of each mind has played a deep, joyful game, and they have been ever more certain as the sonic measure shortens. No sonic flak from elsewhere can deflect them now.

The game is over, and the race is to be won.

As their arms reached around each other, Joe and Kassy felt the shock of each other's reality, of real flesh, of backs and hips. And all other meaning seemed to drop away from them, as they took in each other's faces, each other's bodies. And in a reality beyond the immediate moment, they protected each other. The flames that rose all about them seemed gradually to slow, till each tongue of flame seemed suspended by the stillness in which they alone moved, moved to take their joy of each other, laughing now, warm mouths and bodies slipping together towards a fusion of joy, while the flames were held to a standstill, and all time seemed to empty into a kind of silence.

So for the whales also, the game is over and the race is won. At the first slippery touch, they roll together, sliding into one, moving upwards with growing joy, faster and faster towards the surface of the sea, rising into a different world, higher and higher, the sea now greener and lighter, their bodies pressed together down all their length, their bellies interleaved, caressing and embracing to the sharp point of pleasure, till they break the surface of the sea in ecstasy, erupt into the bright sunshine, leap high above the white foam-flecked waves; explode into a sky of dazzling blue.

And in that other dazzling world beyond time, Kassy's world and Joe's merged into one. And from somewhere deep inside or outside them, an explosion of flame burst outwards and burnt everything to whiteness.

And the old world died forever.

The whales part now and fall back with a massive crash into the sea, rolling under with a last thrash of their mighty tail-flukes, and sink down exhausted but complete, into the unconscious depths, tuned perfectly together now, feeling no more the pain of separation, their souls merged, their minds transmitting one common bright song of joy and triumph to all the distant seas.

By the standards of the universe, by which such things are measured, a singularity in space-time is not such a unique event. After all, black holes are everywhere, sucking in the debris of the universe, pulling in huge stars and planets like our own, holding them for a glorious moment on the sensitive edge of an event horizon, and then drawing them on, where no light can ever escape, into a cosmic shaft of infinite depth, where all creation can be made new.

And elsewhere in the universe, supernovae are exploding, using the unlikely spur of beryllium to stir the right mix of carbon and oxygen in their spherical depths, before spewing them out; holding everything back too perhaps, for a glorious dense moment of savouring, before throwing out the stuff of stars and planets in a shockwave of neutrinos, to seed the universe with an infinite variety of new possibilities for life.

And everywhere, of course, there are huge folds of space-time, with other potential singularities, bending and stretching the expected boundaries of space and time, and sometimes breaking through them, bursting through from one fold to another.

So perhaps this was a relatively minor singularity, though in a significant place. A slight shift in emphasis perhaps; a sliding gear-change across two or three closely similar futures, the final tip-over caused by something, in cosmic terms, as delicate and as gentle as the stroke of a butterfly's wing.

And yet the world has been made new.

CHAPTER EIGHT

FROM FAR AWAY, KASSY HEARD A VOICE.

'Kassy! Kassy, are you all right?'

She opened her eyes. Boff was bending over her. She felt spent, and dazed.

'I think so,' she said.

'I think you must have passed out for a moment. Are you sure you're all right?'

'Yes I think so,' she said.

She tried to get her bearings. She was in the labs and must have fallen to the floor. There was smashed glass and other wreckage around her. Her left shoulder ached. Boff looked concerned.

She looked up at the stool and the white worktops. She could see the dazzling blue sky through the skylights above. It seemed strange to her. She sat up and looked down the labs. The clock stood at four o'clock.

Across the room were some racks for seed trays. They were full to bursting with boxes of growing plants, varieties of wheat and maize, rice and millet. She recognised them all, and yet she was somehow surprised. There were so many varieties. The strong, green shoots were growing beautifully, powerfully. Apart from a few things she had knocked off the work surfaces, the lab was in perfect order. She struggled to get her thoughts together.

Boff was speaking. 'You've been working too hard again. No wonder you pass out. You should be ashamed of yourself. It may be brilliant research, but you'll give yourself a nervous breakdown.' Boff seemed really worried. He was picking up some of the debris from the floor.

'You should talk,' Kassy grinned as she got up. Boff looked reassured, and she sat on the stool at her workplace. There were some papers on the surface in front of her, and she took a moment to try to make sense of them but she couldn't. She was beginning to worry herself.

'I don't know what happened,' she said. She turned to him. 'I think I had the most amazing dream…'

'Never mind that now,' said Boff, 'how do you feel?'

'All right now, I think,' said Kassy. 'I must have fallen and banged my shoulder.' She rubbed it, but it seemed to be only slightly bruised. There were a few mysterious scratches on her arms.

'Do you feel strong enough to come and see Dad?' he asked.

Terror struck her. She looked straight at her brother. 'Oh, no, Boff,' she said, 'I couldn't.'

Boff looked amazed. 'Why not?'

She felt confused.

'Because he won't... he won't agree... with anything... I...' she stopped. She felt really strange.

'Of course he will,' laughed Boff, 'what are you talking about?' She looked at Boff, feeling vaguely suspicious of him, though she couldn't tell quite why. She feared he would side with their father against her.

'What are you worried about?' said Boff. 'Come on...we agreed, Sunday lunchtime. We're not working any more today. You promised...'

He seemed impatient for them to get going.

'Did I promise?' she said; and then, 'What's the time now?'

'It's just after midday.'

Again, she glanced down the labs at the clock. It must have stopped in the middle of the night. Somehow she thought of a full moon rising over the labs.

'Dad's expecting us for Sunday lunch.'

She looked again at Boff and was strangely comforted by the fact that he appeared to be carrying an old basket-weave shopping bag. She looked inside it, and it was full of vegetables.

'Do you think there's enough?' he asked nervously.

She laughed. 'You know best,' she said. Boff was a brilliant cook.

'Come on then,' he said, encouraged, and moved off. She followed him down the labs.

He led the way along the corridor, past the reception area, and out of the main doors of the building. It was a typically hot sunny day with the usual high greenhouse haze. They cut the corner across the grass and then walked down the long driveway together. It all seemed very free and open and she had an odd sense that something was missing. As they walked, she was half unsure of where he was leading her, but she said nothing. She wondered if she might have a mild concussion, but she didn't want to worry Boff.

They went down the Backs, and followed the paths to the wooden bridge over the Cam. There was the hot summer smell of new-mown grass. As they crossed the river, Kassy looked down at the quiet water for a moment, and watched the reflection of the only small cloud in the sky dissolving into the fractured blue. Then, at the edge of the water, she noticed a sleepy butterfly moving in an old lilac tree.

'Ooh Boff... look!' she said brightly, and then felt silly. She'd used that tone often, long ago, when she'd walked Boff as a baby in a pushchair. It was a copy of her mother's tone on seeing something exciting for the children. Yet it was nothing special; blue butterflies were common enough. Nevertheless, she felt mysteriously elated.

When they arrived at the porter's lodge at Queens', Boff led the way through, and across the courtyard. It was still and hot, and somewhere Mozart chamber music was drifting lazily through an open window. At the bottom of one of the ancient wooden staircases a card read 'Professor J. White'. Some garden tools and old wellington boots were half-falling out of a cupboard there. They went up.

Jonas sat in a big chair at his desk, working at his PC. As he turned, Kassy noticed that he had a neat grey beard, which ended in a white point. When did he grow that, thought Kassy, illogically, because then she remembered that he'd always had a beard.

'Hello,' he said. 'Don't mind me. Sit down, both of you. I'll be with you in a few moments.'

He was concentrating on finishing something at his desk. Boff put a long forefinger to his lips in a humorous way, and holding his basket high, tiptoed off into the kitchen like the cartoon cat trying not to disturb the dog. Kassy sat on the worn sofa behind her father and found herself staring at the familiar portraits on the alcove wall behind her father's head. In the middle, directly behind him, was the painting of some old industrialist, long forgotten, his ginger hair almost white, a sad face. On the left was an attractive man with a twinkle in his eye, perhaps a rather seedy writer of sexy bestsellers. And on the right was a blank space. She puzzled for a moment and then it came to her. She waited respectfully till her father looked up.

'There now,' he said, pushing his computer back. 'I can stop for the day.'

'Dad,' she said, 'where's the portrait of Joe Goodman?'

'Joe Goodman?'

'Yes,' she said, 'didn't you have a portrait of Joe Goodman on your wall there?'

'Who's Joe Goodman?' he said, completely at a loss.

'You know, the famous scientist.'

'I don't know anything of the sort.'

Suddenly Kassy felt at a loss too. She felt her father was about to put her down, make fun of her limited knowledge. She fell silent, and turned to Boff who had just come back into the room, but he looked equally confused.

'Didn't he invent… the Superseed?' she said nervously.

Her father's laugh confirmed her worst suspicions. 'Superseed?' he said. 'Where did you get that idea?'

'Well, didn't he win the Nobel Prize for… inventing something… the…'

Superseed? She thought suddenly, what was that? What had given her that idea? She wondered who this Joe Goodman was, and whether it was all something she had dreamt. She stared at the blank space on the wall and suddenly an inexplicable sense of loss swept over her, a terrible sense of her own loneliness, as you might feel after making love deeply and awakening to your own separate being.

'Oh it's nothing,' she said. And it was all she could do to stop herself crying, though she had no reason for it at all beyond this painful sense of separation, sharper than she had ever felt it in her life. She wondered who Joe Goodman was, or where he was at this moment. Though why she should be concerned about him, she couldn't say. She couldn't even imagine what he looked like.

But now Boff was speaking.

'What's the Superseed then Dad? Is there such a thing as a Superseed?'

'Oh yes, indeed there was,' said Jonas, wriggling into a more comfortable position in his chair as if about to conduct one of his history tutorials. 'The search for the Superseed was quite a fashionable notion just before the turn of the century.'

'Did anyone win the Nobel Prize for it?'

'No, oh no. The idea never really took off. It would have suited the big transnationals, but their scientists weren't quite quick enough. Here, let me get you some wine. We're going to treat ourselves today.' He got up and headed for the sideboard, where he got a glass for each of them and started to open a bottle.

'What was the idea of it, Dad?' put in Kassy, trying hard to recover from her sense of confusion.

'Superseed? Well, the idea was to engineer some superior strain of wheat or whatever. Only part of a much bigger process to help the transnationals to corner the market in food supplies.'

'Wow!' said Boff, pulling a face. 'Nasty.'

'They didn't think of it like that. Some really believed it would help the world. It was all part of an accepted way of thinking at the time. Anything was fair game for profit.'

'What stopped them?' asked Boff.

'Aha. Now that's a big historical controversy. I'm having quite a battle with Jorrocks of King's at the moment.' He hesitated.

Boff grinned. 'Go on,' he said. Kassy was mildly surprised. For some reason Boff seemed to be unusually indulgent towards his father.

'Well, Jorrocks insists it was the failure of technology. She says the science turned out to be far more difficult than they thought: too many interacting genes. She says that if the quest for a Superseed had succeeded, it would have led to a whole different world. But because there were so many companies with half a Superseed, they fell fighting among themselves, and so the idea of diversity came in by default.'

'And what do you say?' asked Kassy. Perhaps she knew already but she couldn't remember.

'I accused her of being an old-fashioned Western reductionist.' He chuckled. 'She was really insulted. It's obvious to me that the failure of the Superseed idea was the positive contribution of the so-called Third World.'

'Third World?' asked Boff; he looked quite attentive.

'Yes, that's what they used to call the countries that were exploited at the time. That or "underdeveloped". Sounds a bit patronising now. But there was a general refusal to follow the discredited model of Western "progress" which had only ever helped the rich elites. It's a very complicated picture, but they took a united stand, brought in land reform, replaced export crops with crops for local consumption, gave the countryside priority over the city, stopped the patenting of seeds, and eventually expelled the transnationals. It was hard to begin with, but paid off in the end. The "Food First" movement helped of course, and the concepts of sustainability and diversity. Ah, but concepts – that's where Jorrocks accuses me of being a "Neoplatonist psycho-historian"! I did laugh. The article was in *History Tomorrow* last week.'

'What's a Neoplatonist whatever?'

'Well broadly speaking, someone who thinks that ideas come before facts.'

'Does it matter that much?'

'Oh, it's probably very minor stuff,' said Jonas, 'but it matters to us historians. Just as scientific method matters to you. But I do think ideas are more important that Jorrocks thinks. They can become tomorrow's mass assumptions. The nineteenth-century idea of technical progress became the twentieth century's mass assumption; and the twentieth century's ideas of ecology have become ours – especially the idea that food is not just for profit, and that the soil must be improved and not exploited. That's turned out to be important. When the climate changed so suddenly, and knocked the world back so tragically, at least the ideological basis was there to cope with it.'

There was a pause.

'Well,' laughed Boff, 'apart from all the infighting, what are you working on now, Dad?'

'Not much in that line,' said Jonas happily. 'Since I've fin-ished the big histories, as you know, I've been taking a bit of a break from it: working with Bradwell in the village, rebuilding those barns. But lately I do find myself drawn back to the millennium years. It was a fascinating time. So I think I might be on the verge of writing something about it. They only just saw the danger in time. Did you know, in those days only a tiny fraction of people worked on the land, factory-farming it to provide cheap food for the billions who lived in the cities. The irony was that so many city people were either unemployed or unproductive.' He snorted humorously. 'Now thankfully the vast majority of people give at least some time every year to sustaining and improving the land. And the cities are getting smaller, instead of bigger. No, it's a very imperfect world we live in, but at least now no one in the world starves...'

'Then it's all been worthwhile,' thought Kassy, and found she'd said it aloud.

'All what?' asked Boff.

And Kassy thought: Yes... all what?

Boff was looking at her strangely.

'Have another drink,' said Jonas, and got up to refill their glasses with his favourite wine. 'Bradwell's forty-nine,' he said.

As he was pouring, Kassy's eyes wandered to her father's bookshelves. All his own books were there, along the top shelves, a row of them: the best standard works on the twenty-first century, especially *The Struggle for Land*, *The Climate Crisis* and the latest, recently published *Towards a Sustainable World*. She had read them all. He was one of the most respected historians of his time; and yet quite unspoilt. Perhaps because he was so happy doing what he did.

As he filled Boff's glass, he said, 'I hear you've brought our meal today. I can't wait to see what it is!'

'Come with me, Dad,' said Boff, and led Jonas off into the kitchen. After a moment, Jonas came back.

'Wonderful stuff he grows,' he said, rubbing his hands together. 'I've left him to make it.' He grinned and settled into an armchair near her, and looked at her.

'Tell me how your work's going, littl'un.'

A slight flicker of disapproval ran through Kassy, and she wondered why. He had always called her littl'un, since she was a child; it had never troubled her before. He didn't really mean it in a patronising way.

'It's fine Dad,' she said. 'Still working on salt tolerance for the local farmers. Nothing especially exciting. Oh yes, one thing out of the ordinary. I made a call to Tanzania this week on the Agrinet Free Seed Exchange. It seems they have a small area in the east with surprisingly similar soil conditions. We might be able to help each other out.' And she started to explain, doubting if her father would really be interested.

But like all local problems that concerned her, it seemed to fascinate Jonas.

The meal was a relaxed family affair, but something Kassy always enjoyed. They sat around the little table and had Boff's vegetables and Jonas's own bread and the wine and some local peaches. Jonas grew nostalgic remembering the fruits of his childhood.

'I don't suppose you remember tinned pineapples,' said Jonas, 'with plenty of syrup. Or bananas! Now there was a taste. I'd enjoy a banana right now.'

And they all laughed because they knew how impossible and dreadful it was.

Kassy felt slightly embarrassed, feeling that somehow she should have contributed something, but Boff made her excuses, and explained how she had passed out at the labs. Jonas seemed very worried then, but she was able to make light of it, explain that she was just a bit tired.

'But of course you would be,' he said. She wondered why. She was certainly feeling rather strange, and she found herself more and more an observer of their talk. Boff and his father loved to question each other's assumptions, and the conversation crackled along on all kinds of topics. Sometimes it was some matter of local politics, for example when they discussed the possible closure of the mathematics lab to the public. It had been a great craze at one time, and people would pay to watch the strange attractors unfolding holographically in different colours and dimensions. But mathematics had moved on so much, Boff thought, and the exhibition had become outdated. Then sometimes the talk moved on to more personal matters; Boff was missing his girlfriend, who had been away helping her family at their farm, but would be returning later that night. It occurred to Kassy, perhaps for the first time, that she had become very important to his life.

Dad, of course, declared he had been a lonely old bachelor now for many years since their mother died, but he seemed content enough. Nobody asked about Kassy. They seemed to take her happiness for granted and she didn't want to think too much about it.

Later, after lunch, they opened another bottle, and Jonas sat on the easy chair, while Boff and Kassy shared the sofa. Now, the conversation broadened again and they talked of religion and God and the new worship of the goddess of Gaia, and all the little cults of local places which Jonas explained were part of a rediscovered tradition that went back to the Greeks and Romans and even long before. And Boff, with his knowledge of whales, talked about the sea goddess and the goddess of the moon who, they had believed, ruled most of the Planet Sea between them.

But Kassy found she couldn't add as much to these conversations as she would usually have done. Perhaps she really had been overworking lately; she certainly felt quite unusually tired. Now they were talking about whether divine intervention was possible in the world and what form it might take, and her concentration drifted away again. But not long after, she heard again the name of Joe Goodman. Boff was asking her how this name had occurred to her and Kassy couldn't answer. Jonas couldn't place the name either, so Boff went over to Jonas's PC and picked out the biggest scientific encyclopaedia he could find in its memory and started to look through. It took only a few seconds before Boff was reading aloud, for the benefit of the others.

'Goodall, Goodban, Goodly – ah, Goodman,' he read, 'one or two Goodmans. Sir Eric Goodman, of course, the atmospheric chemist. George Goodman – he was a chaologist, Mayor of Manchester in '24... ah, here we are, Joe Goodman. Yes, it's the only one; Joe Goodman. Is this the one, Kassy?' He read on, silently for a moment.

Kassy felt irritated. 'Well, go on,' she said.

'He was a biochemist... Born 1960... various degrees... er... worked on various cereal cultures... nitrogen fixation...

etc, etc… Not much about him. Ah. His research was lost when he was killed in an accidental fire in his laboratory. So the inquest said. It says here: Speculation at the time suggests that it could have been suicide… while of unsound mind… er… Discoveries in this field were later made independently by… oh… several people… at Sussex and… er… cross references… That's all it says. There. Obviously not one of the significant figures in world science.'

'Don't make judgements too easily,' warned their father. 'Comparative significance is a minefield.'

There was a sudden silence. Kassy's shoulder ached from when she had fainted on the lab floor.

She wondered how her mind could ever have come up with that name. Joe Goodman. Very strange. She tried to consider its associations; where she might have heard it before. A minor scientist who had died in a fire over fifty years ago. There was only that blank space on the wall. It meant nothing to her now. A blank space. Well, it brought with it, perhaps, the smallest stab of nostalgia for a world long past and gone. But that was all.

And suddenly she wanted to go home.

Because the effect is disturbing. As if one moment you were standing in a peaceful wheat-field on a warm summer's day; for all you know everything is solid and reliable: the warm earth, the reassuring hum of a distant tractor; but then there is a vast seismic shock and obliquely through a split in space-time surges an alternative world, forcing its way in from some deep and secret place beyond time. The old field is violently removed and another field slipped in, a quite different field, instantly replacing it. *And though you can still hear the hum of that same distant swarm of bees, you are disturbed by a sense of deep unease, as if a cloud had crossed the sun. But you have no idea what makes you uneasy, because with it, of course, has come a change of perception, as if the old field had never been.*

Such a singularity may open a vast rent in the fabric of time and then close it again, almost as if it had never happened; so that it causes hardly a ripple on the apparent surface of time, quite easily forgotten. A parallel world has been shunted sideways into unbeing, so you might never know what you may have gained, or what you may have lost forever.

But until the aftershocks of such a singularity have quite settled, the effects can be a little disturbing.

A slight sense of déjà vu perhaps. A yearning for something you can't place. A doubt over a name.

And yet the world has been made new.

'No, it was a stupid idea.'

Jonas was talking about the Superseed, and Kassy's mind must have drifted away for a moment. Even Boff had given up a spell of playing devil's advocate, and Jonas was holding forth a bit now, as he sometimes did. It was the middle of the afternoon and time to be going, but she felt indulgent towards her father. She glanced out of the window, across the age-old Cambridge courtyard where a diagonal shadow was moving imperceptibly across the warm stonework. Jonas was in automatic lecturer's mode.

'… but all of the patent legislation in the world wouldn't work where there are millions of smallholders, instead of a few rich farmers…'

He's getting old, Kassy thought, looking at the white hair over his ears. And does he notice when he repeats himself?

'... but we always have to be careful that those sorts of monolithic ideas of domination don't take hold again. We must always be vigilant...'

He doesn't look vigilant, Kassy thought, he looks half asleep. And a moment later his eyes were indeed closing.

'... of course, that's not to say Kassy, that genetic engineering hasn't helped us all quite a lot...' His head was back on the pillow of his big armchair. 'Here and there... As one idea among many...' He was drifting off.

'That's the thing... diversity...'

He was asleep.

Kassy and Boff glanced across at each other and smiled.

'I think it's time to write a little note,' said Boff.

This was a routine accepted now between them all. Rather than disturb their father, Boff wrote a little note of thanks, while Kassy kissed the old man on the forehead. He stirred, but he didn't wake, and they tiptoed out, while Jonas went on snoozing in his favourite chair.

'Dear old fellow,' said Boff when they reached the still warmth of the courtyard. 'It's funny to think he was a rising star in his youth. I found an article about him the other day from the Sunday papers in the '20s. He'd stuffed it into the back of one of his books. Talked about his amazing executive ability. Said he was destined to be one of our future leaders.'

'Why wasn't he?'

'I expect he found he was happier doing what he really wanted to do.' Boff grinned and added, 'Aren't we all?'

'How's your work, Boff?' Kassy asked, 'I'm sorry, I never asked.'

'Oh me – I'm as happy as I could be. I'm preparing for my trip to the Atlantic. We hope to go as soon as we've helped to get the harvest in. This time I think I'm really going to make sense of it all.'

'How do you mean?'

They were walking through the town now. It was still only teatime and the midsummer sun on the houses gave off the comforting scent of warm brick. Boff took off his jacket and started skipping down the road in his shirtsleeves, like an eccentric puppy. Kassy ran after, laughing, to catch up.

'I think,' he said, 'I'm on the edge of a breakthrough… You know my collection of whale-sound translations? Well, there's no problem about the richness and the variety of their culture. That goes without saying now. But the new breakthrough, I'm certain of it…' and he stopped now and looked dramatically at her. 'The next step is to understand their view of Time.'

'Oh Boff, what will you dream up next!'

'No, seriously. The whales themselves are so incredibly curious about us, I think it won't be long before we can communicate properly with them. It's trying to find a way to match their deeper unconscious with our sharper consciousness; that's the problem in a nutshell. But I'm beginning to think that the intentions they have are in some way independent of time. Maybe… maybe it's an incredible survival mechanism that evolution has worked out; can you see it? Just suppose they can see into the past and into the future. Now – for them, there is no definite future, only an infinite number of possible futures, all of which they can consider. So then they can send out their powers to influence the future they need. Like the old concept of prayer, but more developed. Maybe… in their generosity, they can choose the future that's best for all of us…'

Boff turned in his excitement, and Kassy stepped back against the wall. She could feel the heat of the bricks through her shirt.

'Perhaps they're intervening all the time and we'd never know it.' He held his long hands up to his cheeks and his eyes grew big.

Then he shrugged and moved on. 'Or perhaps they only intervene when they're desperate… Anyway, Kassy, it's my life's work, I know it, and if I can find out just a small part of the answer before I die then my life will have been worth something. The Nobel Prize, here I come,' he said, and he danced off ahead of her down the street.

Kassy couldn't help laughing at his absurdity.

'You've had too much to drink,' she said.

When they got back to Danby's shop, Ginnie met them at the downstairs door. She had just arrived back from her parents', and her bike was in the corridor next to Kassy's. Ginnie was an eccentric, passionate-looking girl whom Kassy had met only rarely. She had only moved in with Boff over the last couple of months. Kassy had a sudden desire to get to know her better, and she agreed to share a cup of the local tea with them before she set off home.

She went up the stairs. The familiar living room was very much as she remembered it; the big wicker chair, the sofa, the carpet hanging from the wall, were all in the same places, but here and there Ginnie had begun to put her personal touches on it: a new picture, an extra noticeboard above the desk. It was cool and tidy though; most of the real clutter of Boff's life was confined to the bedroom at the back. Kassy wondered if Ginnie had been able to make much impression on that. But Kassy didn't stay long enough to look. Much as she liked Ginnie, and her shyness and her sudden high laugh, she was nevertheless anxious now to get back to her own home. She soon made her excuses and picked up her bike in the corridor downstairs. She took out her battered yellow hat from the saddlebag and crammed it on her head.

'Nice to see you Boff,' she called to her brother, who was sitting on the stairs to see her off. 'And you, Ginnie.'

'Go carefully,' said Boff, and grinned. He got up and joined Ginnie at the top of the stairs, putting his arm around her. Both were smiling as Kassy wheeled her bike out on to the sunlit street, and she waved at them briefly as she set off on the familiar route out of town, to her cottage in the country.

The sun was dropping lower in the sky as she came up the slipway on to the old toll road. The sign read 'YOU ARE LEAVING CAMBRIDGE', and she felt the familiar lifting of the spirits as she left the town behind her. The long straight road lay ahead. It would take her perhaps an hour or more to get home, but she was used to the journey and enjoyed it, especially in the long summer evenings. She loved commuting to the town to work, and living out in the countryside, though most people did the opposite. Often the most useful ideas might occur to her as she cycled in of a morning, or on the way home at night. There was the occasional lorry, though seldom on a Sunday, but there were other cyclists too on occasion, sometimes flocks of them, and she would get into conversations with them as they cycled along. But the road was deserted now. She avoided the cracks, and weaved among the occasional tufts of grass.

As she rode, she watched the familiar fields on either side, rich with all the variety of life she remembered from her childhood. Once she had even travelled this way in a car – the last that her father had owned; she would always remember the excitement of that extraordinary experience. Some of the old apple orchards had survived to this day but they were smaller now, as farmers were beginning to experiment more with vineyards and olives. There were fields of maize especially, and wheat and barley and rye; permaculture estates; fields laid to clover and beans, big red tomatoes of uneven shapes, sunflowers growing tall and meadows with Anglian Whites and Friesians, and new breeds of cows whose names she didn't know. There were woods of many different kinds of trees, and hedgerows full of wildlife. She heard the chattering of yellowhammers and the occasional straying seagull. And as she worked her way up the long slow rise, somehow the uneasiness of the day started to slip away from her, and she felt more awake, and also more at peace with herself. Her shoulder was a lot better; it seemed to grow easier with use. She stopped at Peter's farm for a few minutes and bought some eggs and bread, and chatted with the farmer's children there who were growing so tall these days, especially Tom. She was near the top of the rise now and as she put her purchases in the basket of her bike, and rode back on to the road, the phrase 'Give us this day our daily bread' occurred to her, for no particular reason, except that she felt thankful for the warm smell of the earth rising from the grassy verge by the hedgerow, and for all the life around her.

After the brow of the next hill it was flatter and easier, and there was only one more slight hill to go. This was her favourite moment. She would toil up to the crest, ease up around the bend and, as the road dropped away, there it was: the Cambridge Sea, like a dark blue smile across the horizon, lying still and smooth in the afternoon sun. And as her bike sped down the gentle slope, with its wheels whirring faster and faster, she could feel the breeze full on her face and taste the saltiness of it, the taste of childhood and freedom.

After she had left the main road, it seemed only a short time till she arrived home. She dismounted at the gate, and walked the bicycle down the drive between the fruit trees till she came to the cottage. And there she stopped, watching for a moment the sun warming the grapes on the front wall. Everywhere was perfectly still and perfectly at peace.

She moved on round the house, wheeling the bicycle, and again she stopped to take in the old aspen tree at the corner of the house. She laid the bicycle against the side wall of the house and, before she turned the corner into the back garden, she looked up again at the poplar. Very high up, the leaves rustled and glittered in the evening sun, and she looked for a long time, taking in the sun slanting across the top of the tree. Suddenly she heard a scrabbling sound. A squirrel was running along the apex of the roof and then down the tiles, and she saw it leaping across the blue sky into the poplar tree which shook and shivered its triangular leaves in the evening sun. She had a strange sense that she was sharing this beauty with someone. It was almost like being in love.

And suddenly, she had a sense of what would happen next. She would turn the corner of the house and go into the back garden. And there would be a little lawn behind the house, and the rose arch and the vegetables growing and the greenhouse. And at the edge of the little lawn would stand a man with his back to her. For a moment he wouldn't realise that Kassy was there, and he would stand there while she took in the dark hair curling at the back of his neck, slightly touched with grey.

Then at last he would turn and he'd come over towards her.

And she'd say cheerfully, 'Hello Joe.'

And he'd come over and put his hand on her tummy.

'How's the baby?' he'd say.

And all at once it would be complete.

CHAPTER NINE

AND SO SHE TURNED THE CORNER.

It wasn't at all like that, of course. In a way she was relieved. It didn't matter that as yet there was no husband, or child. She loved this place. She felt safe. It was like an island of safety that she would never want to leave. She'd never regretted moving home, and was quite happy living on her own.

She went back for the bike and took it round to the shed. Then she took the shopping from the basket, and let herself in by the back door. She unpacked the bread and eggs in the kitchen, and for some reason decided she would make herself an omelette for supper. Her mind rested, while her hands went through the familiar motions of cooking. Afterwards she took the omelette upstairs and, her memory a blank, sat on the bed with the plate on her lap. She listened to the comforting sound of the wind turbines across the field, the regular whipping sound of their blades. And then, as she ate, she looked out of her bedroom window, enjoying the last of the evening sun across her garden, on the rose arch, reflecting brightly off the greenhouse roof.

She was content enough.

Then the strangest thing happened to her, which she remembered almost all her life. As she looked idly out of the window, she was certain that she could really see, for a fleeting moment, a man standing in her garden, leaning on a spade, as if he'd been digging a trench there. He stopped and looked up to her, and she knew this man. Standing in front of the wide crack in the earth, he looked up at her with such love, and pain, that she was struck as if by lightning. He seemed so much to want to reach out to her, to say something to her, but the divide between them was too great.

Then he dropped to his knees in front of the hole in the ground and slowly he seemed to fade out of her sight. As he faded, he shrivelled and crumpled up like a baby, and then dropped into the hole in the ground, which was almost the size of a grave. And at that moment there was such a terrible cry of pain, and longing; so that in response, she even found herself forgetting everything, and running downstairs and out into the garden.

But of course, there was nothing there. A blank space. The buzzing of insects. A few cracks in the dry earth. Nothing at all.

Kassy remembered this daylight dream, as she called it, long after she married and had the girls. Just occasionally her mind returned to it at private moments, when she looked down from her bedroom window on the still evenings. And then would come that strange sense of closeness mixed with that undefined sense of loss which made no sense to her at all. Or if somebody brought up the subject of supernormal experiences she might mention the vision of the man dropping into the ground, though no one ever seemed to be able to offer an explanation. She could even joke with Timothy that this was really the man of her dreams, and she had a vague idea that he had a name though she could never remember what it was. It was all so unreal. In the event, it was the only experience of its kind she ever had. She supposed it had something to do with the pressure of her work at the time; which, though satisfying, had also been very demanding. After all, she had even passed out that morning in the labs, she had been working such long hours.

Once or twice she talked about it with Boff; but of course he had this obsessive interest in alternative worlds.

'How can you be sure it wasn't a real person?' he would say. 'Perhaps he came from an alternative reality, which you denied him. Or which he sacrificed for you. Who knows?'

And his eyes would open mysteriously wide, and his long fingers would flicker about expressively, so that Kassy couldn't help smiling.

'No seriously,' he would say, 'or how do you know it was *your* dream? Perhaps he's the real person and you're in *his* dream…'

And Kassy would laugh, knowing what would come next.

'Or perhaps,' he would say significantly, 'or perhaps… the whole of what we call reality is just the dreams of whales, playing with alternative worlds.'

He'd always bring the whales into it somewhere. Kassy thought that Boff grew more eccentric and absurd with every year that passed.

But her interest in that little moment faded with time. It wasn't important. She was busy with her family, and successful in her work; life was rich and diverse, and she had less and less time for dreams.

* * *